BERSERKER
GREEN HELL

BY

LEE FRANKLIN

For Marcelo. This is just the beginning.

Australian born Author, Lee Franklin, now resides in the idyllic Yorkshire countryside with her incredibly supportive husband, Marcelo, and three boys. After 10 years in the army, working as a personal trainer and logistics officer, Lee found her true calling elbow deep in the blood and gore of horror writing.

Penning diverse stories Lee's flavour is usually seeped in action horror and creature features. An avid reader across the genres, Lee also enjoys running, coffee and dogs in no particular order.

Stalk her here!!

Website - www.leefranklin.com
Facebook - @LeeFranklinAuthor
Twitter - @WordPilgrim
Instagram - leefrank1979
Goodreads - www.goodreads.com/lee-franklin-writer

Chapter One

Hell?

Why had I come back? I asked myself for the millionth time. *Because you're a coward,* came the familiar answer. Because I'd returned willingly to this purgatory, and trudged up and down all nine rings of Dante's Inferno. Trust me, I wish it *was* the pit of fire and brimstone the preachers all promised.

I wish it was a place you could leave, or a nightmare that would leave you—but it's not. Hell is an endless green; broken only by deep shadows, white blankets of rain, and cesspools of bog and mud. It's a thick, viscous heat that rots body and mind with incessant, stagnant decay and the odour of sweating men—and that's so bad we can't even stand our own stench. This is where we are: in Hell—or *Dia Nguc* as they call it in Vietnam.

A lot of us blokes got the call up—but I signed up.

The first time was to win Jenny's family's respect. The second time was because that didn't work and, well, I had nowhere else to go because I'd lost my place at University. Mostly, though, I couldn't handle watching Jenny's belly grow with my best mate's baby.

Bullets don't give a shit what colour skin you got, and for all its sins the military doesn't give a fuck either; you're just a number they will chew up and spit out regardless.

Swirling black spires of smoke could be seen from six klicks out—that's *kilometres* for the civilians. Within two clicks it penetrated the jungle with long, reaching fingers and we could taste the oily ash of it in our mouths. Burning bamboo, rice paddies, gunpowder, and the subtle, distinct smell of burnt flesh thickened in my nostrils as we swept in from the outskirts of the village.

It was the rice paddies we saw first; black, smouldering ash with a sheen of oil marbled on top of the water—green crops wouldn't burn without it. The Viet Cong didn't have oil, or flamethrowers, to waste on crop fields. We spread out wide under Hammo's instructions, close enough to see each other through the smoke, with bandanas pulled up over our faces so we could breathe.

We were a handpicked group of specialists—unwanted oddities in reality—and we rolled in to do our job, which was to try and make sense of this shit storm.

The brutal, dry heat of the fire battling with the humid air sapped our strength as we sloshed around the edge of the paddies looking for the road in.

There's always a road in.

We didn't expect any action, of course; we were just *The Ghosts*, *The Reapers*. We were unofficially attached to whatever grunt/infantry unit was in the area, and reported informally to some unofficial JAG team. Our job started after the bullets stopped flying; we went in to collect dog tags, MIAs, KIAs, and inspect for any potential war crimes. The whole fucking war was a crime if you ask me, but nobody ever did.

Lance Corporal Azzopardi dropped to his knees. We all followed like we were in a Mexican wave. Wog-Boy, like me, was into his second tour. You could tell by the lines of disgust and profound sadness carved into his face, the way his eyes narrowed in a perpetual squint of shrewd analysis—but mostly it was the trembling, always the trembling. As I made my way over, his fingers pointed toward the ground. "What *is* that, Pinny?" he asked me.

Now, I'd spent all my summers with my Mother's mob—the Wardandi people of the Noongar Nation. My Uncle Miro taught me to track with my cousins, which became my specialty and my VIP invite to this particular shit-party. We Aboriginals aren't known for much more, perhaps drinking and football.

Wiping the sweat out of my eyes, I watched as the jumps and jitters ran down my comrade's arm to the muddy earth as he pointed to a significant depression in the boggy ground.

Studying it carefully, I replied, "That there is a

bloody large U.S soldier, Wog-Boy—see the typical GI boot tread? Going on the length of the print, he must be close to six or seven-foot-tall and maybe around one hundred and twenty kilos—weight is hard to gauge in this bog. Thank God he was running away from the village." I cast about for further prints but was unable to find anything obvious in the smouldering marsh. "Are Yanks meant to be in this area?" I asked, "I thought they were further north?"

Americans made me nervous, and with good cause.

On my first tour, back in '66, I'd been detached to an in-country training wing to instruct the scouts on tracking techniques. I'd just come out of the latrines one evening when I heard shouting around the back. Being a nosey bastard, I poked my head around the corner to see some LT and a group of cronies surrounding some poor Negro who was kneeling on the ground.

The LT was forcing him to lick shit from his boot.

I didn't have any rank to pull to stop it—but I did have a fist-sized rock.

I lobbed that rock over my head and heard it clatter on the tin roof of the septic tank. I called out *grenade!* and watched as everyone threw themselves to the ground. In any normal situation, nobody would fall for that ruse, but in Vietnam, everyone was twitchy. Hell, I almost dropped to the ground myself.

The LT, Karey, (I found out his name later) stumbled and fell through the roof of the septic tank—eat shit indeed, sir.

After that, LT Karey's victim, one Sergeant Marcus Hawkins, and I became best mates—until he left the war two months later after friendly fire took a chunk out of his leg.

Karey, on the other hand, eventually went to prison for war crimes after taking the lead role in a village massacre.

Marcus and I would write letters to each other; he just loved to fill me on all the happenings back home. It was Marcus who told me that the year after, when the M16s got handed out, some three hundred yanks had been killed by friendly fire—that's in *one* year! There's the consequence of armed, untrained conscripts burning their boredom and demons with a heavy mix of drugs and alcohol.

While I continued casting around for more prints, Taz squelched in behind us on his short, stumpy legs. He pushed his thick glasses up on his piggish nose, and I heard the click and grind of the camera as he wound on the film. It was a top of the range Minolta SLR—provided by the JAG—and thankfully the only kind of shot we'd heard that week.

Taz was a long way from shooting family photos at the local shops back home in Tasmania. Flat feet had him running errands for the Head Honchos back in Nui Dat until our last guy kissed a mine—then Taz got re-posted to the Reapers.

It's a hard task out there for any desk jockey pogue, but Taz took it all in his stride. Pushing his mop of black hair out of his face, he had Wog-Boy stand next to the footprint for reference.

We were an odd mix, but it worked as well as it had to. None of us were sure what we were achieving, or even what we were really doing out there. But we were keeping someone up top happy, and I had a paycheck, so that was just fine with me.

There were no more prints, certainly nothing definite I could make out in the slush of ash and mud. I gave Wog-Boy the sign and we all continued moving on.

Even though that monster footprint was headed in the opposite direction, my hand gripped just a little tighter on my rifle. *Why would a bloke that big run away from a fight?* I asked myself. *Because something bigger, or meaner was on the other team,* came the unwanted reply.

It didn't take long for us to find the road in. It was not really a road, more of a wedge of dirt between the paddies that was just wide enough for a cart. We rolled in single file and approached the wrecked remains of the village. I immediately got to work and started casting about for any prints or tracks that could tell us a story.

Some huts were still burning, and amidst the normal miasma of death and fire there was a strong smell of bleach in the air. I had noticed it before at previous sites, but this time the acrid stink was that much stronger.

We didn't normally hit a site so soon after the main event and it had us all on edge, so we moved fast. I cast about and indicated to Hammo and Taz the familiar GI tread in the churned up mud and mess around us. I estimated at least ten soldiers had been through the village, clearing out each building as they went.

"Hammo, Taz, come take a look at this," I called over, confused by what I'd found.

"What is it, Pinny?"

"Are US Marines in the habit of taking their boots off and running around barefoot?" I indicated a clear trail of prints belonging to someone—or something—that easily reached over six feet tall and about one-fifty kilos.

Hammo removed his glasses and wiped them semi-clean on his filthy shirt. "What the fuck? This doesn't make sense."

"Look, there's more," Taz called out as he set his camera off snapping and grinding.

I followed the trail but there was no discernible pattern to it. While the GI boot prints were like following the yellow brick road—predictable standard operating procedure—the barefoot prints were chaotic and cut a winding, looping trail through the carnage of the village.

By now, I'd identified that there were at least two, maybe three different prints—each one running, jumping and walking sporadically. I chose one to follow and threaded my way through the village, trying to recreate the movements. I kept tripping up on arms, legs, and largely unidentifiable body parts that were strewn about the place. Corpses decorated with their own long, coiling viscera lay still in stagnant, muddy piles—one sat propped up against a pig's pen, a dark black and red void where his jaw had been torn from his skull. The hairs on the back of my neck prickled up.

I followed the tracks into a hut. I felt a crunch under my foot and I gazed down to the hard-packed mud beneath my feet. A scream caught in my throat. It was the body of a baby, too small to have been born, its tiny head smashed open onto the dirt.

My stomach rolled and I turned to vomit in the corner of the hut's remains. But I couldn't stop myself before the bile arced in the air and splashed onto the body of the infant's mother. Her stomach had been torn open and swarms of fat flies converged on the congealed blood in a convulsing wave of black. On her chest, there were two large, weeping red wounds where her breasts had been sliced off.

"Holy Mother of Christ," Doc moaned as he stepped forward to close the mother's glassy eyes—her poor face was contorted in terror. I watched as he scraped up the remains of the infant the best as he could and laid it gently in her arms. Doc had been a Priest back up in Queensland; he crouched next to the bodies for a few moments to whisper a prayer and pay his respects of sorts. Doc was a good man, gentle— an old soul, as my father would say. He clung to his God with a vice-like grip in the jungle, never once rising to anger or hopelessness. He had the same powder blue eyes as my old man, and that self-same anguish burning at their core. I recognised the grief. It was buried deep away to be dealt with another time—or perhaps, as in my dad's case, never.

I put my rifle down and laid my hand on Doc's shoulder in the way of support as I tried to find words to console him. As usual, I came up with nothing. As with most blokes of my generation, talking about our feelings just wasn't a thing.

"I know in war people die, soldiers die—and die badly. I expected that. But this? This isn't war, this is *madness*." Doc spoke so softly I only just caught his words.

"It's madness alright, Doc, and it's getting worse the further north we head. This is the third village we've seen like this in as many months. Ain't nothing much you and I can do about it—if this is what they do to their own people." I tasted the bullshit in my own words.

Doc shot me a look as he stood up and peeled off his rubber gloves. The sweat that had pooled in them spat across the room. "You really think this was the VC?"

13

I couldn't meet his eyes so I stared at the horizon instead. I recalled the scuffle of prints outside, and unless the VC were wearing size ten GI boots, or had doubled in size overnight, then no. "Fuck man, I don't know." I hawked a wad of smoky phlegm from the back of my throat out through where the hut door had once stood.

"Why would the US be doing this shit, man? It doesn't make any sense." Doc swung his arm out around at the village as he walked away. "This isn't war. This is just mindless bloody slaughter."

Our section head, Hammo, sent us out in pairs to clear what remained of the huts. I had seen enough and looked no closer than I had to. Puddles marbled with blood and mud told a story that was no fairy tale.

Everyone I found was dead—violently dead. It was not the kind of death that women, young children, and old men should suffer. It was a massacre.

What remained of the bamboo huts had been peppered with rounds. I pocketed a few casings that belonged to AK-47s, and some I didn't recognise.

We cleared what remained of the huts. Doc followed through behind us, checking pulses—if there were places on their bodies left to check, that is. A few of the bodies had been shredded by gunfire, but most had been *butchered*.

Eyes burnt into my back, somebody—no, *something*—was watching, waiting. The mood

14

grew dark and ugly amongst us as we all picked up on it. And, as usual, there was nothing we could do. Nothing we were meant to do, just gather pieces of a puzzle for some other schmuck to piece together.

An explosion from behind us made my guts lurch before I heard it. I was hot on Doc's heels, all eyes out, as we swarmed towards the position. We found Hammo limping away from the dust and smoke.

"Booby-trap," he grunted. He clamped his hands over his ears as blood trickled out onto his jawline. With his coke-bottle lenses cracked and knocked askew, he winced in pain as he showed us all the mangled flesh of his calf.

"Well, that's a one-way ticket home, Hammo." Doc sighed as he threw his medic kit on the floor and set to work.

A sudden rattle of automatic weapon fire broke out in the village; bullets whined, thumped and tore chunks out of the wreckage around us.

Launching ourselves into the quagmire of mud and gore, we searched desperately for any form of cover.

I saw a flash of blonde hair as Snowy popped his head up first. A bullet kicked up dirt in front of his face just before he rolled away. I watched him indicate two shooters: nine and eleven o'clock. I passed it along the line before I crawled towards a pile of bamboo to take cover.

Hammo and Chook were well back with Doc,

who was bandaging Hammo's gaping leg wound the best he could with his stomach flat to the ground.

Chook squelched and fired off into the radio.

Wog-Boy waved at me from the remains of a hut across the way; he had Stevo and Macka tight on his ass.

Snowy was behind the hut. Taz and Cam crouched behind me on my left hand-side, flat up against the side of a pig pen.

Stevo and Macka shuffled forward under our covering fire so they could use the M60s to full effect.

The SLR kicked my shoulder like a donkey in retort.

A blood-curdling cry broke out, and in the corner of my eye, I saw Snowy getting pulled in under a bamboo screen. He was kicking and ramming his rifle at someone behind him, but just couldn't shake him. I started to make my move over to him when I heard Taz scream out, *"GRENADE!"* over the *ratta tatt tatt* of the rifles.

As I hugged the dirt, the explosion punched my insides, and I lay there unable to breathe. White dots flashed over my eyes as I watched Snowy's mop of white-blonde hair get pulled below that screen. Helpless, I couldn't breathe, and I couldn't move. A hand grabbed my shoulder and dragged me back to the side of the building just as a bullet bit the dirt in front of me. My stomach unravelled, and I was able to grab a mouthful of air. Within seconds, despite my aching ribs, I was back to it, and I watched Wog-Boy and Taz scramble over to help Snowy.

I leaned against the hut, still trying to catch my air. I couldn't believe my eyes when a mountain of a man sprung out of the haze of smoke. He screamed with bloodlust, and his lips peeled back to reveal a set of chipped, stained horse-teeth. The whites of his eyes glared as he tore towards us with his body jerking as our rounds slammed into it.

Without pause or hesitation, the big guy flew straight into Cam's unsheathed bayonet. At close to six foot, and one hundred kilos of hard, rugby muscle, Cam was not a small fella, but this man—this aberration—bulldozed through him and his bayonet like they weren't there. He drove them both into the ground with a massive thump of flesh.

Cam grunted in pain as I ran over to heave the other man off him. I could see the tip of his bayonet poking through the man's lower back, and the multitude of red flowers blooming on his shirt where he'd been shot— but he was still trying to choke Cam to death with his huge, meaty hands. I lifted my rifle and fired two shots straight into the side of the big man's head—that finally did the trick!

I wiped his blood off my face and checked on Cam.

Blood splattered, pale, and gasping for breath,

Cam gave me the thumbs up as we stared in shock at the soldier.

He was Vietnamese, and dressed in rags like a farmer; as with any of the Vietnamese we encountered, he could easily have been from either side. He was ludicrously massive for a local—who would typically average five foot nothing and fifty kilos soaking wet.

The footprints must've belonged to him.

The man's face was a picture of devastation. It was torn, shredded, and threaded with half-healed scars—those landmines were a bitch. It was the stink of him that turned my guts inside out, though. He smelled like someone had just shat in a bowl of straight bleach.

Shaking my head in disbelief, I helped pull the dead weight off Cam. I then raced off to where I last saw Snowy with Wog-Boy and Taz.

Snowy was curled up in a ball in the corner of the trench where he'd been dragged. He was soaked in blood, and I saw his bayonet slick with the stuff and shaking in his hand.

Wog-Boy lay exhausted with blood splattered on his face and massive welts on his forearms where his rifle sling hung around their attacker's throat. It looked just like he'd had garrotted the Vietnamese guy until Taz could make the killshot with a double tap to the head.

As with the other guy, this one was unusually large for a Vietnamese; he was punctured with at least ten stab wounds from where Snowy had stuck him like a pig. His ugly-ass face also looked as if it had been kissed by the same landmine as the other big bastard.

"He wouldn't die, he wouldn't die," Snowy repeated as his blue eyes blazed with shock in a stark contrast to the thick curtain of blood that coated his hair and face. I pulled him out of the hole. Wog-Boy wriggled the bayonet out of Snowy's grip while I called out for the Doc.

"Wog-Boy, we gotta evacuate now! Let's hustle!"

Hammo roared. "The bastards are going to light us up—the Yanks are coming in."

Ice-cold sweat broke out down onto my back. With was no time for questions, it was time to haul ass. I grabbed Snowy by the shoulder, pushed him forward, and shouted at him to run. We then followed Hammo, who was draped between Macka and Stevo. Chook took the lead back through the paddies towards the treeline, and made it only about five hundred meters before we heard the roar of the F100 tearing through the sky.

Where the hell had they come from so quickly? Ragged and exhausted, our adrenaline kept pushing us deeper into the jungle as we prayed we'd make it.

The air was sucked out of my lungs moments before the searing heat engulfed our bodies. Skin tingling as my nerve endings were singed, I was encased in a ball of heat...

Pain was a good sign; any burn past the nerve endings in your skin was bad news. When you felt *nothing,* your flesh was melting off your bones, your body was shutting down through shock, and you were seriously fucked up. I gasped for air like a drowning man, but found nothing but hot carbon monoxide that seared my lungs; all of the oxygen and moisture in the air was instantly vacuumed up by the voracious appetite of the napalm.

Stumbling, I pulled a shocked Snowy along through the undergrowth, as the black dots that swam in front of my eyes grew larger until they dominated my vision.

Finally, I fell unconscious to the floor.

I don't know if it was seconds, minutes, or hours until I woke up, but when I did, my skin was wrapped taut and hot over my body, and every breath rattled painfully through my scorched lungs.

Moans of agony echoed all around me. I jerked my head up to see Woody, a tall lanky fella from Intel, wandering lost through the jungle. He was only fifty meters or so behind the leading group, and his clothes had completely incinerated. All exposed parts of his flesh bore a weird look of white leather as he stumbled around aimlessly before eventually collapsing on the jungle floor.

I heard Doc flitting about, his voice low and calm as he checked on each of us. I watched his shoulders slump as he walked over to where

Woody had last been seen.

Struggling to my feet, I checked out my body as I converged with Hammo and the rest as they made their way in silence. With his injured leg, Hammo had pushed Macka and Steve ahead of him and had been closest to the back with Woody. Most of his hair was burnt off, and ugly blisters covered his back. Still, he was alive and incredibly high on Doc's precious stash of morphine. He was one lucky bastard indeed! Thank fuck they hadn't used phosphorus in that bomb, or none of us would have made it.

Chook was about one hundred meters in front of us and had to backtrack. Never had I seen the young fucker run so fast.

"Did you call that aircraft in, Chook?" I asked.

"No. I had no chance to. Only found out they were coming because I picked up some American channel."

I saw that his radio was still intact, and he was already calling in a situation report. His face grew even paler as he relayed information to Wog-Boy.

With Hammo doped up on morphine, Wog-Boy had suddenly found himself promoted into a complete cluster-fuck. We were on the wrong side of the valley, and the area would be inaccessible for days. With a forty kilometre trek around, we would not be making our rendezvous.

It was time for a plan B.

"Okay, boys, we're rolling out in thirty minutes. Get your shit sorted and see Doc if you need to. Macka, Cam, I need you boys to make a stretcher for the boss man here." Wog Boy indicated the stupefied Hammo.

"Pinny, I need you on that map. Work with Chook to find us an extraction point—or at least a medivac for Hammo. Taz, you and Snowy run an ammo and ration check, and then try finding some water. Then we'll get the fuck out of here."

Chook and I managed to organise the medivac. The best access for a bird was ten kilometres North West through the scrub, and to a small plateau. We had twelve hours get there for a pickup at 0700 the next morning.

It was Hammo's best—and only—chance. We would then have thirty-six hours and a fifteen kilometres trek south for a vehicle pickup for ourselves.

Chapter Two

The location, a small, cleared plateau on the rise of a small hill, was secured. We spent the morning forging our way through a kilometre-wide clearance zone, before hunkering down and facing out.

We popped a smoke grenade and waited for the bird to zero in and scoop Hammo out of there. Secretly, I thought he was a lucky son of a bitch, and I'm certain I wasn't alone on that one.

It wasn't long until we heard the reassuring *wokka wokka* sound of the blades from the Iroquois helicopter overhead. The bird swooped and hovered as Doc got him harnessed in the stretcher and all ready to be winched out of the war.

Hammo had just made it about a hundred metres up when all hell broke loose. I caught sight of the tail of the RPG as it tore through the metal flesh of the helicopter to send the bird into a crazy downward spin. I watched the resulting maelstrom of destruction like a rabbit caught in headlights, and with everything in slow motion.

One of the gunners sitting on the helicopter's door took the gamble to jump free of the bird, but the large front rotors sliced him across the shoulders; it cut the poor guy in half like a silk ribbon.

Struck dumb, we all watched helplessly as Hammo's stretcher whipped around beneath the hapless bird at a radial velocity the human body is just not designed for. I lost sight of him as he was plunged back into the top of that green hell, as the chopper churned up the canopy behind us. The bird continued to spin before it hit something solid enough to lurch it in our direction, and without the need for discussion, we all made to leap down the side of the plateau.

The jungle rippled out towards us just before the shockwave kicked me in the solar plexus and carried me bodily from the lip of the gorge. Aviation fuel roared in a huge, blistering explosion, and flickering tongues of orange flame blotted out the endless green as we rolled down the side of the steep embankment like sacks of meat and bone in some ghoulish pinball machine. I landed near Cam just as a thick, leafy branch exploded through his stomach. I watched him writhe around like an insect on a pin, as bright red blood bubbled around his lips.

Smoke billowed through the foliage. It stung our eyes and wrapped its long, tendril fingers around our hacking lungs until we were doubled up coughing and heaving thick, black phlegm.

It was at that moment that all of us surrendered to the unrelenting green-black shadows of hell. Resigned, we waited for the *rata-tat-tat* that would shred our brutalised bodies to pieces and finally bring us some respite, and we waited for the shadows to spring to life with demonic, white grins of rage that would accompany the mad bludgeoning of our weary remains with the dull, rusted blades of indignant revenge.

Searing pain rippled through my body as it throbbed and ached; my mind was devastated by the sheer waste of human life—but death did not fall upon us, only the rain, that chill bearer of mush, and the lifeblood that fed our Green Hell.

The scratch and squawk of the radio burst into life as Wog-Boy called us in. Bruised and battered, we lumbered in, glad that the smell of burning fuel and smoke had mostly overwhelmed the stench of burning flesh; I didn't think I would ever eat roast pork again.

Wog-Boy and Stevo were re-checking the map and arguing furiously when we got there—war can fuck up your mind faster than a line of bad coke.

"Macka," barked Wog-Boy, "we need to secure this location. I want eyes out—get over there on my six o'clock, facing out. Pinny, get over here. Confirm our location. Stevo, give Pinny the map and get on my three.

Doc, I'm on my way."

"Why does the fucking Abbo get the map?" Stevo whined. Stevo, a thickset rugby player topped with a flame of ginger hair, was essentially a racist bastard—he argued *every* point Wog-Boy and I made.

"Cos, I need you to go do what you're good at— lifting heavy things," Wog-Boy barked.

"Well I guess Abbos are only good at reading picture books," said Stevo. He rolled his broad shoulders and unceremoniously pushed the map in my face. Playing forward for the district rugby team, Stevo was built like a brick shithouse, and had a brain like one too. But, like Wog-Boy said, he was good at lifting heavy things and swung that M60 around like it was a candy cane.

"When was the last time you read a book that had nothing but pictures in it?" I asked Stevo. Of course, I knew full well that in addition to his M60, he lumped around a decent amount of wank mags in his pack.

"Fuck you."

"Nah. I might be your type, but you sure as hell ain't mine." I smiled. It was also known that Stevo's dick and his mind were in constant conflict. For as much as the big guy berated the Vietnamese, he couldn't keep his hands off their women; he eschewed all the Western skin shops for the young—and often underage—ones of the East.

"Just get us the fuck out of here," he growled and stalked off.

Taz lay facing out. His face was unreadable, his thoughts impenetrable. Chook, hunkered up next to a tree, pale as milk and still waiting for his first shave, was rattling a trail of codes backwards and forwards over the radio to no response. Doc was busy breaking the tags off Cam's neck before trying to bag him. We were now out of bags.

Snowy was a shivering wreck. His eyes were wild and rolled in his head as he sucked on his cigarette with furious intensity. Doc had managed to clean most the blood off his face and hair, but water was limited so his skin was still smeared with the stuff. Usually so cool and calm, Snowy's thin, corded muscles reminded me of a whip—yeah, the kid was like a whip with white-blonde hair, bright blue eyes, and a cheeky, boyish face; I guess that's what made him the ladies' man of the group. It saddened me seeing him so rattled. He was young—just twenty, I think—and it was his first tour. I really didn't think he'd see the end of it.

I sighed before settling down over the map. It was a total shit fight. We were a two-day forced march away from where we should have been, and closer to the Yankees' Alpha Zero Five One area of operation.

Nobody wanted to be near the American GIs—they were more trouble than they were bloody worth.

Five minutes later, and Wog-Boy was standing over my shoulder while I recalculated our position for the third time and hoping to get a different answer. I ignored the jerks and tics of his tense body as he tried to stifle the trembling that belied the air of confidence he was so

27

desperate to exude. Wog-Boy was three months into his second tour and, up to that point, still refused to yield to the shellshock tremors that possessed we lesser souls—that never-ceasing, inexplicable heart-in-your-throat kind of terror that made a body shudder, its bowels want to purge, and caused random ice-cold sweats. Getting rat shit drunk or choofing a fat joint made our bodies forget the quivering—at least for a little while.

Wog-Boy was moulded for war, a second-generation Australian from a brutish Maltese family; he carried his

"Dago" chip on his shoulder as a badge of honour and wielded his parent's self-same fury and fierce temper; he'd often break into an avalanche of abuse in a mix of Italian and Maltese at anybody who crossed him.

I didn't hide my parentage, but I didn't advertise it either. My mum died giving birth to me, and while I inherited her dark brown hair and eyes and well-tanned looking skin, I mostly passed as white. Living with a white dad, it was an unspoken agreement between us it was just easier that way.

"Where the fuck do we go, Pinny?" Chook asked as his radio squawked and squelched; there was absolutely no signal to be found.

"We need a high point," Wog-Boy stated the bloody obvious.

"Well, we're only half a click out from where

we dropped the smoke," I said. "But there's no way we could climb back up the way we came down. Besides, I don't really want to head in the direction of where that RPG came from. So, if we head south east here, there's a large hill or something only six clicks away. I think it's meant to be Yankee territory." I pointed at the map, and Wog-Boy followed my finger to the converging lines on the crinkled paper. "There's the American Area of Operation—in the valley on the other side. We should get something up there."

"Damn Yanks," cursed Wog-Boy, "more dangerous than the fucking Viet Cong with their friendly fire." He smirked at his favourite old joke. "Alright, guys, we've only got two hours of sunlight. Let's hump out of here before our friends with the RPG decide to come looking for survivors."

For the next day and a half, we covered ground as fast we could lugging our sixty-kilo packs. We took turns to lead as we forged a hacked path through the jungle's Wait-A-While vines with our dulled machetes.

Up and down rocky gorges, crossing creek beds—it was painfully slow, and a fucking mess.

Doc stayed close to Snowy who had, by all accounts, gone tropo—jungle-crazy in Aussie-speak—and was next in line for a ticket home. Chook fiddled incessantly with the radio, scouting the airwaves, but getting nothing but silence and the occasional squelch.

The further we struggled up the hill, the less I could hear the birds and monkeys that usually filled the jungle with their broken cacophony. The eerie muteness was broken only by Snowy's sporadic outbursts of jabbering and the thwack of our blades tearing at the almost impenetrable flesh of that green hell. The silence of the jungle itself was deafening, and seemed to suck the sound out of anything else.

Numerous times, as I scraped and tore my hands and knees climbing up the rocky ascent, the hairs on the back of my neck prickled to attention. Ice-cold stones settled into the pit of my stomach as I sensed us being watched—not by the Cong, but by something far more primal. I felt vulnerable, exposed.

I felt like prey.

Alert, as I watched the rest of the section, I noticed their knuckles taut, white with strain as they gripped their rifles ever tighter, and their eyes scanned out deep and into the shadows and the dark canopy above us. I occasionally caught flickering movements in my peripheral vision; they'd quickly disappear into the green haze that surrounded us, and they filled me with a sick sense of dread.

All my instincts screamed at me to flee back down, to beyond where we'd come from, but my head just told me my nerves were shot and to ignore them.

I caught up with the rest of the group as we

finally reached the plateau. The canopy was slightly thinner there, and it let through random shafts of sunlight and tantalising wisps of fresh air. Exhausted and sodden with sour sweat, I still had that annoying ache in my belly telling me to run away. After catching my breath, I approached Wog-Boy. He stood over Chook and scrambled through the channels like some madman as he tried to make contact.

"Hey, Wog-Boy, this place feels all wrong man," I said, keeping my voice low. "We need to get out of here—I have a bad, bad feeling."

Wog-Boy just glared at me. Although he was irritated to be interrupted, he didn't scoff at me as I'd expected; the nervous flicker in his eyes told me he sensed it too.

Before he could answer, the silence was filled with a shrill shriek of terror.

"*Doc!*" we both yelled and turned on our heels to run to where Doc had been tending to Snowy. We tore through the jungle, and what should have taken seconds seemed like forever as the grasping green hands of that hell grabbed onto us. The wet crashing sounds of vines and saplings exploding around us filled the jungle as everyone ran to help.

Macka got there first. We found him kneeling next to Snowy, who was curled up in the foetal position, eyes rolling as he babbled in incoherent grunts and whimpers.

I ran past them with sweat as cold as ice water

trickling down my back as I charged on in the direction of Doc's scream. Somebody tackled me from behind and heaved on my shirt. I crashed down, winded, with my arms flailing in the air.

Swearing loudly at my unknown assailant, I opened my eyes to realise there was nothing beneath me... I'd almost fallen off the edge of a cliff.

"Bloody hell, Pinny," Macka muttered. "Look where you're bloody going." Macka was a crazy kind of kid, but he had a good heart about him.

I rolled over onto my back, struggling to catch my breath, as Macka stood up and tried to wipe the thickest of the mud off his pants. "Thanks, Macka," I spluttered.

I rolled back onto my stomach and crawled forward to the edge of the cliff. There, I saw a trail of broken, and bent plants, which, along with deep gouges in the soft mud, indicated precisely where Doc had gone.

"Do you think he fell, Macka?" I asked as I struggled to my feet. I saw he was looking down at something on the ground with a puzzled furrow on his dirt-smeared brow.

"No, I don't, Pinny. Check this shit out," Macka replied. I bent down next to him, and my stomach dropped at the sight of the oversized footprint in the mud. It was at least double the length of my own size nine boot, and the print was twice as wide as my own. Whatever had made the imprint must have weighed in at well over two hundred kilos! However, what made my stomach curl in sick terror were the four-inch claw marks raked into the earth around the print.

In all my years tracking, the only time I saw anything like this was when I spent a few years running crocodile hunting tours in the Northern Territory—where I met Jenny. Some of those crocs were huge bastards, but nothing like what I was looking at. Whatever made those claw marks wasn't a croc—certainly not on the top of a hill, and with no salt water for miles. The length of the print told me this *thing* moved on two legs— any four-legged animal with feet like that would trip over itself. I had to admit that those claws and the sheer size of the prints scared the crap out of me.

Macka called out for Wog-Boy. Wog-Boy came at a jog, but stopped short when he saw the look on our faces. "What is it, boys?" he asked. "Snowy is as crazy as a cut snake—we can't get a damn straight word out of him."

Macka pointed to the footprint. "Doc didn't fall, Boss."

Wog-Boy glanced down, and I saw his dark olive complexion go white as the moon. *"Xi iz-zobb u dak!"* he grunted in Maltese. "I mean, what the *fuck* is this shit?" Wog-Boy asked us, scared and angry. "Is this some kind of fucking joke? If it is, I'm not fucking laughing. I thought you said this was American territory."

"No, boss, we aren't fucking around," Macka answered. "This is just something we found."

"According to the map, it *is* American territory. Boss, there ain't no predators in Vietnam that would leave a track like that." I mumbled, as if any of it really made a difference. "Not any animal in the world I can think of, actually."

Wog-Boy swooped in to get a closer look at the weird print, when Doc's shouts and screams from the bottom of the hill split the air.

"Holy hell, the poor bastard's still alive," Wog-Boy gasped. "We have to go after him."

Macka and I exchanged a glance. We were terrified, but we knew Wog-Boy was right. We had to get down there and try to save him, it's just what you do.

Wog-Boy called the rest of the troops over; Stevo went pale and Chook vomited at the sight of the massive footprint. Snowy, already a blubbering mess, didn't even seem to register it at all—his whole body just kinda trembled. First Cam, Doc, and now Snowy. We were all headed straight for the white jacket.

It took mere moments for Wog-Boy to organise us.

Chook would sit with Snowy on the plateau and keep searching the airwaves for contact. The rest of us—

Stevo, Macka, Taz, Wog-boy, and me—had twenty-four hours to enter the valley, rescue Doc

34

and get our asses out of there.

We descended slowly down the hill. At times we just slid through the mud, other times we'd climb and half-fall. All of us were spaced out in a staggered line, so should anyone slip, they wouldn't take out the man below them.

Internally, I argued the logic of what we were doing, but I knew deep in my heart this wasn't about logic—it's just about your mates. Logic had left this war before it had even begun.

Once again, good old Uncle Sam had drawn we Australians into a war of ideological bloodshed, against an enemy as invisible and lethal as the reasons for being here. I'm just as guilty, though, I came back. I came back hoping to find the answers to questions everybody threw at me when I went home.

No, I didn't.

I came back here to hide.

I couldn't handle it—Jenny with Simon's baby. Was Jenny happy? I hope so, I still loved her. Yes, some hells were easier than others; here at least, and for all my sins, I belonged. I stepped on Doc's bush hat, but before I could share my discovery with the others, we heard more screams from below us; shrill cries so filled with terror that I actually pissed my pants. Me, a grown man of twenty-odd years, halfway through my second tour! I stopped in my tracks as the hot, strangely comforting stream of piss ran all the way down my leg and into my boot.

35

Too scared to even register the shame of having done that, I followed the others' faster pace down the hill.

Once more, I was slipping and sliding in the slick ground, and for once, I was grateful for the rainy deluge that washed away the bitter smell of my fear.

We lowered ourselves further into the dense jungle with no idea of what to expect.

Chapter Three

Before we knew it, the ground levelled out in front of us. We fanned out around the head of the trail, B rifles raised and fingers twitching on triggers, as we peered out through the grey slab of rain and impenetrable jungle.

No movement, no sound, no visibility. For better or worse, we moved forward, spread out, back-to-back.

Each one of us looked out over the tops of our scopes with nervous, paranoid eyes. It was painful and slow going, but that's the only way we were prepared to go, what with the owner of that oversized footprint skulking somewhere out there.

A darker shade of grey streaked across my point of arc. Macka reacted as it entered his, and the silence exploded into the booming of his rifle as he emptied half a clip into the thick shadows.

Wog-Boy thumped him in the side with the butt of his rifle, "Cease fire! Cease fire!" he yelled.

At the moment he turned his head, a dark, looming shadow lunged out of the rain and slashed at Wog-Boy's face as it hissed and growled like Satan himself.

Macka kept his finger on the trigger and fired round upon round in the shadow's direction until the thing faded from view with a pained, howling roar and Wog-Boy collapsed against him. Poor Wog-Boy was a mess—his face nothing more that bloodied stripes of torn, ragged flesh; five distinct, jagged lines ran diagonally from an inch past his hairline, all the way down to his chin.

"What the fuck was that?" Macka hollered as he scanned the jungle. Reaching into his webbing, he grabbed his bandages and deftly bandaged up Wog-Boy's face the best he could. The bandage was soaked wet through with blood and rain within seconds. "Come on, Boss, you'll live. You'll be uglier than a hat full of assholes, but that's gonna be an improvement anyway,"

Macka joked—humour in adversity was very much the Australian tradition.

Macka tried his best to conceal the trembling of his hands and the blood splashed on his clothes as he helped Wog-Boy to struggle to his feet.

"Let's keep moving—find Doc so we can get the hell outta here," Wog-Boy growled through his pain.

With Wog-Boy badly injured and suffering from the onset of shock, we'd inched forward only a few metres before the rain stopped, the humidity sucked steam off our clothes, and a thick mist filled the spaces in the jungle the plants couldn't reach.

A guttural, primal roar echoed through the jungle. An ice-cold knife twisted in my stomach, and my fingers sat twitchy on my trigger as we edged forwards, back to back.

This was a bad fucking idea.

Still, we stumbled onwards, and just about all I could hear was the maniacal pounding of my own heart. A thunderous *whoomp* echoed out from the trees above us, and a thick rain of leaves and snapped branches cascaded down on top of us. Then came the distinct sound of somebody being punched—a soft, wet noise—followed by a winded gasp of shock. I noticed the absence of someone by my side, the lack of body heat, the breathing, and the jostling that comes with being so compact.

"Taz!" I shouted as my knees turned to jelly. I spun around just in time to see my friend's body hurtle up towards the canopy at tremendous speed. He let out a blood-curdling scream as he jerked and jarred through the branches until he was out of sight. Above us, the canopy trembled furiously, and leaves and branches showered down. Taz's camera landed with a soft *thump* on the dank leaf litter beside me.

Then there was silence.

"Where did he go, Pinny? *Where the fuck is Taz?!"*

Wog-Boy screamed.

"I dunno, man!" I was trying to keep myself together; my eyes were desperate to see through the dense foliage and up into the canopy above, and my stomach was lurching. *It could have been me! He was right there on my shoulder!*

"*Bullshit!* He was right next to you!" His face paled and his eyes widened with fear as he scanned the canopy.

Macka and Stevo alternated between keeping their rifles pointed out and towards the canopy. I could smell the raw fear stinking up their nervous sweat—it was pungent as all hell, and I didn't fucking blame either of them.

The canopy shuddered as it purged itself of Taz's body.

He fell to the ground like a sack of potatoes, landing just ahead of us with a resounding *thump*. He was bent up all unnatural, twisted, and fractured; bright bubbles of blood frothed around his mouth, all thanks to the massive puncture wound in his chest that sucked in the sticky jungle air. I threw up in my mouth a little as I saw what could only have been the pink-white shimmer of spine where it had been pulled out through his body.

Raucous laughter broke out above us, and it chilled me to the core. Wog-Boy grabbed Macka, who had keeled over to puke his guts up, and shouted at us all to move.

Staying alert for any movement in the canopy above, we did as ordered as our training kicked and bypassed our thinking. Although, I don't think we were ever trained to deal with whatever the fuck was up there in the jungle canopy.

A loud roar rippled through the trees ahead, so we moved in the opposite direction—back towards the hill.

Whatever the fuck that thing was, I wanted as much ground between it and us as possible.

"What the hell was that, guys?" Stevo whispered between labored breaths.

"I dunno, and I don't *want* to fucking know," Macka snapped.

As for me, my brain was racing over a million miles an hour as I desperately grasped at any plausible explanation. "I heard US troops reported seeing a Bigfoot type creature in the interior. A *Batutut,* they call 'em here—or Rock Apes," I said.

Stevo's eyes bulged at me.

"Some of your fucking cousins then?" he snarled.

"Where the hell do you get all this crap? You do talk a lot of shit, Pinny."

I shrugged my shoulders. "I read stuff other than titty mags," I mumbled. "Do you have any better theories?"

"Would one of those apes match that footprint you found, Pinny?" asked Wog-Boy. His voice was weak and he looked like shit.

I thought about it for a few more moments as we waded through the jungle. Then I shook my head. "Nah, that thing would be too big to be climbing about in trees." I shivered as I remembered the details of the print; those large, raking claws weren't designed for climbing. "I think the print we found was more reptile than primate."

"So, you're saying there's two different animals *and* the fucking VC hunting us?" Macka snarled.

"I guess so... well, *maybe*. Actually, come to think of it, I don't think Batutus are arboreal." My stomach sank as I realised what I was saying.

"*Arboreal*— what the fuck does that mean?" Stevo snapped.

"So Bigfoot, Lizard Beast, and something fucking else is out there? Anything else you'd like to add to your fucking fantasies?" Macka laughed.

"I'm just trying to help."

"Well, shut the fuck up. You're not helping with your fucking fairy tales."

It started raining.

We moved as fast as we could, as our lungs strained to siphon oxygen from the damp air that swamped us.

Forcing our way through the undergrowth, we came to a small clearing. Although visibility was limited, we could not have missed the horrific spectacle twenty meters in front of us...

Strung up in a twisted knot of a tree, no more than a few meters ahead of us, was Doc. He was spread-eagled in some a gruesome parody of his Jesus on the crucifix.

Our comrade swung there, still very much alive and whimpering in agony, with blood gurgling from his mouth in hot pink bubbles. His chest had been sliced open, and his ribs cracked wide apart to display the bloody, raw mess inside.

Stunned with disbelief, Macka stepped forward as he attempted to make sense of the horrific scene in front of us.

Then came the audible *click* of a tripwire and Doc exploded.

Blood, flesh, and gore rained down on us, and splintered shards of bone sliced through our clothes and skin miniscule razors.

It was at that point that I simply quit functioning.

Everything I could see, smell, and hear was entirely incoherent; my brain slid into slow motion, my body numbed, and I slumped to the ground. I stared down at my hands which were thick with grime and peppered with bone fragments— *Doc's* bone fragments.

I saw Stevo shouting wordlessly and firing his gun into the canopy, yet I couldn't hear the boom of the rifle that brought down the shower of leaves. Trails of blood wept from his ears and down along his jawline to give him crimson sideburns, as his face contorted into madness.

My ears began ringing; the internal noise was deafening. I folded in on myself, trying to block it out. A hand gripped my shoulder, trying to get my attention. I looked up to see Wog-Boy's bloodied, bandaged face just centimeters from mine. He was shouting at me.

As I turned, I saw Macka smack Stevo hard in the head with the butt of his rifle. Stevo collapsed to the ground, and the barking of his gun was silenced once and for all.

The world spun around me. The acrid, bitter stench of gunpowder filled the air, tinged as it was with the cloying, metallic stink of fresh blood. I pulled a bloodied lump of Doc's flesh out of my hair, and then puked as I tasted a sweet saltiness in my mouth that I was pretty sure was not mine. I refused to look up to where I knew the remnants of our comrade's arms and legs hung limply from what was left of his mangled torso, which flapped like a tattered flag in a stiff breeze.

With Stevo silenced, Macka succumbed to his own terrors. He hid his head between his legs with tears streaming down his face. To my left, Wog-Boy, hands raised in supplication, was begging his God to spare us from this hell.

His God either didn't hear, or, like the rest of the world, just didn't give a damn about us.

We were broken, defeated men. They'd told us we would be heroes... *bullshit!* I was amongst some of the bravest men I knew, yet after bearing witness to so much brutality in that horrific war, there we were—traumatized and feeling like failures.

We'd seen more than our fair share of the torn up, mangled corpses of innocents—bodies that had been savaged by rabid beasts rather than neighbours from over the border, and we knew all too well we were only there to take notes to pass back up the chain. Somehow, that didn't feel like enough anymore.

Before long, Macka wiped his eyes and stood up.

Wog-Boy quit praying, and they looked at each other with a firm resolve I didn't feel— maybe I was the only strait-jacket candidate one amongst us?

I'm not sure how much time passed before Stevo finally began to stir, but he awoke groggy and clutching the side of his head; his words were slurred like he was pissed as a gnat.

The movies never show it how it really is— everyone thinks that a smack to the side of the head from a rifle butt will give your enemy just enough time to drag you away to their lair where you'd awaken as fresh and re-invigorated as if you'd enjoyed a power nap. The simple truth is, though, the longer you are out—the more your brain has been jellied.

Stevo sat up with the entire right side of his face hanging limp and droopy-looking; it kinda looked to me like it had melted. He grunted in pain, leaned over, and expelled what little remained in his stomach.

Holding him in my arms, I tried to keep him awake, but he lost himself to sleep's embrace with scratchy, gurgled breathing and fluttering birds for a heartbeat.

Macka came over and checked on poor Stevo. "What do you think, Pinny? Will he be alright?"

"Your guess is as good as mine. You pegged him pretty good."

Ashamed, Macka hung his head. "Yeah, I don't know what came over me. I just couldn't handle it, you know?"

"You're all right, mate. I probably would have done the same. He lost his mind, man, and you were the only one with enough mettle to take control." I tried my damndest to comfort him.

"Yeah." Macka was clearly not convinced.

Wog-Boy, whose bandages were a filthy shade of wet crimson, stood up and said, "Let's make a stretcher for Stevo and get the fuck out of here."

"That's crazy, boss, Macka responded. "We have an hour of sunlight left at best, and we don't want to be a third of the way up that hill when it gets dark. We'll kill ourselves for sure,"

"What? You want to stay down here? With that... thing, those... *things* that did that to Doc?" Wog-Boy pointed at the wrecked remains of our comrade.

"It'll get us here, on the hill, wherever the fuck and *whenever* the fuck it wants to," Macka argued. "Let's find somewhere to lay low for the night and get the fuck out of here in the morning. Pinny, what do you reckon?"

He drew me into the debate.

I shrugged my shoulders; I wanted to run—

run like crazy away from that place. But Macka, although he was not generally known for being the brains of any operation, was right: trying to climb that hill at night was pure suicide.

"Let's hunker down here for the night, and give Stevo a chance to recover," I replied. "That way, we don't have to lug his sorry fat ass up that hill."

For the first time, we saw a crack in Wog-Boy's tough exterior. "But I'm the *boss*!" he whined like a petulant child. "You guys have to do what I order you to do... and I'm *ordering* you to get your fucking asses up that hill!"

Macka cocked one of his thick, roachy eyebrows at him. "You're going to play *that* card now? Fuck off."

Wog-Boy spat on the ground. His phlegm landed dangerously close to Macka's feet. "So, I have to wait here like a sitting duck, just because you decide to take out one of your own men by knocking him fucking senseless?"

"I didn't *decide* anything. I acted." Macka fired back.

"Unlike you, who just sat there blubbering like a baby; I just did it, okay? He could have killed any one of us."

Macka stood up, toe-to-toe, with Wog-Boy.

Towering over the guy, Macka was long and lean—he'd been recruited to play for Footscray Football Club in Melbourne, before he got the call-up. I fancied the odds on Macka winning any physical encounter with Wog-Boy, but whilst I liked the kid, I actually had a soft spot for Wog-Boy. I could sense things escalating, but we had enough people to fight, let alone each other.

Forced to act, I slid out from under Stevo's unconscious body, stood up, and put my body between Macka and Wog-Boy. "Alright, boys! Shut the fuck up!"

I broke their standoff. "We now have far *less* than an hour of sunlight left. Wog-Boy, you go get stuff to make a stretcher—so we're ready to leave before first light.

Macka, go find someplace away from..." I refused to look up in the trees. "... *here*. I'll stay with Stevo. Go!

Piss off—both of you!"

Like a naughty little kid caught in his Mom's panty drawer, Macka's eyes widened and his jaw dropped.

Wog-Boy's lips pulled tight and thin in protest, but nonetheless, he grabbed his rifle, swore under his breath, and stomped off in the opposite direction.

Exhausted, I unslung my rifle and slumped back beside Stevo's crumpled body. I cried then—big, wet, sniffling, snotty tears. A heavy, crushing pain tore at my chest as I struggled to keep the sobbing and wracking gasps to myself; I missed my dad more than ever at that point, even though he'd never understood why I signed up in the first place.

"You're a lot of things, but you're not a fighter, son."

He'd told me. "Remember how many times I had to pick you up and dust you off every bloody time you got a beating?" He was right, of course; I'd spent my entire childhood trying to avoid any and every type of physical confrontation. It never worked, though, as I was the perfect target for *Boong* bashings from my classmates.

And my cousins would beat me up for being a *Lamington.* It all fucking sucked, but it was what it was.

What nobody seemed to understand was that the punches hurt a hell of a lot less than the loneliness.

Eventually, though, I'd met Jenny, and she loved me.

She was someone to fight for.

Dad tried his hardest to talk me out of it. He knew I wasn't ever going to be good enough for Jenny's old man—even if I became Prime Minister—but I wouldn't listen. I wouldn't fucking listen, and now there I was in the middle of the fucking jungle babysitting a one twenty-kilo racist bastard who, on any other day, in any other situation, would love to pound the black shit out of me.

My old man would stand me up and remind me that I am as good as—if not better than—those pieces of shit.

He would then tell me how beautiful my

mother was, and how she was the pride of her mob. He would tell me how her laughter would fill up the house. She was sharp as a whip too, and would never let anybody put her down. Dad would often say I had her smarts, but she had more balls than me. Yes, I missed my old man; he tried his best for me.

It wasn't long before I heard Wog-Boy's excited voice. He'd returned from his excursion much sooner than I'd expected. "Where's the map?" he demanded.

"Gimme the map!"

I pulled the carefully folded map out of my pocket and threw it at him.

"What's up, Boss?" I tried to read his face beneath the bloodied bandages.

Wog-Boy walked over to me. He seemed a tad less excited, and more curious. He pointed at the map.

"Look, there's nothing there,"

"Yes, I know that, Boss," I tried real hard not to roll my eyes.

"Well, how come there's a six-foot cyclone fence decorated with barbed wire only forty meters away from us?" he asked.

"What the hell?" I scrutinised the map. There was nothing on it at all on it to indicate an installation of any kind. "You're shitting me, right? Might it be some old deserted Cong village or something?" I tried to reason.

"Nah, mate, this is brand new, shiny American

stuff,"

"What brand new, shiny American stuff?" Macka enquired as he entered the little clearing. He held aloft a metal fence sign that read in both English and Vietnamese: Property of the United States of America.

Trespassers will be shot on sight.

An explosion destroyed our excitement.

The blast couldn't have been less than two hundred meters away; it hit us hard and rolled through our bodies like a runaway road train. Crouching down together, we instinctively huddled around Stevo as shots rang out in an intense firefight around us.

It took me a few minutes to realise I couldn't make out the report of the Viet Congs' AK47s, nor did I recognise the *rat-a-tat-tat* of the other weapons as they thrummed out a vicious assault on my eardrums. But, I did recognise the familiar, thunderous growl of rage that sent shivers all the way down my spine.

With night crawling in and visibility down to about ten meters, we could make out very little—except for the staccato rattle of guns and muzzle flashes from deep within the foliage. The best we could do was keep our heads down and stay huddled in the dirt.

A dark shadowy figure exploded through the jungle and raced by us. At almost three metres tall, it bulldozed through the undergrowth, splintering small trees and bamboo thickets like they were matchwood. I couldn't make out much detail of the creature, other than its sheer size and brute strength, which seemed to be the form of something slender, bipedal, and unmistakably reptilian.

Another explosion. This time much closer—so close that it all but rocked the flesh from my bones. I saw the beast flounder as the explosion sent it reeling backward, until it came to an abrupt halt with its arms and legs flailing. An immense net descended upon the thing's stunned form, and closed in tight.

A group of oddly shaped men launched themselves from the jungle. Leaping upon the creature, they screamed out a battery of shrill war cries and threw their misshapen bodies on top of the beast as it hissed, screamed, and roared at them in angry frustration. The men hung on without fear as their bodies were whipped and slammed around—they reminded me of the clowns on the horns of a rodeo bull— just how they managed to stay put was beyond me. The strange men snarled back at the creature as their battle lust peaked and that net grew tighter and tighter.

As I looked on, another platoon of soldiers converged on the creature. They emerged as if from nowhere and moved with the confidence and precision of professionals—they were most likely commandos. Their weapons were slung, and each one of the soldiers carried long poles with hooped rope at the end. These, they looped around the necks of the men atop the beast to pull them off like they were Animal Control with a street dog.

There was just something about those guys I couldn't quite put my finger on. They were so much larger—in both height and bulk—than the guys riding rodeo on the giant creature, and there was just something about the way they carried themselves that struck me as just plain *odd*.

The commandos appeared oblivious to our presence, which I was more than happy to maintain. There was a silent, mutual agreement amongst my comrades and I that we were not there to be our heroes—we were witnessing something we shouldn't have been privy to.

Instinctively, we moved back deeper into the jungle, with the angry bellowing of the improbable beast covered up any sounds we may have made as we dragged the still-unconscious Stevo along with us.

Six quad bikes rumbled into the clearing ahead of us. They attached the captured beast to four of them, and proceeded to haul it through the cleared jungle, back in the direction it had torn through. The other two quad bikes followed behind in solemn procession, which, in turn, were trailed by three or four soldiers carrying the metal poles. It was almost impossible for us to see anything by then, as the spotlights from the quads bounced off in the opposite direction, while the commandos pulled that hellish beast away.

"There, ya'll are!" boomed a loud American voice as we were suddenly blinded by a piercing spotlight.

We had been so distracted by the capture of the creature that we hadn't noticed a group of the soldiers fan out and come up from behind. My heart stuck in my throat as that harsh light burned into my fatigued eyes, and without discussion, we all raised our hands in the air in unequivocal surrender.

"Y'all tha group of Australians with tha' coupla buddies ya left up on yon' hill?" he barked at us in his thick, southern drawl.

I nodded my head; there really seemed no use in denying anything at that point. I knew these guys were meant to be our allies, but deep in my gut, all my alarm bells were ringing. Dropping out of our faces, the spotlight left us blinded and blinking against the sudden darkness.

"C'mon up, y'all git now. Let's get y'all back to base—we'll fix ya somethin' to eat."

The southerner tugged on Wog-Boy's arm to pull him to his weary feet. I heard one of his comrades radio in the find—namely us—as seven huge soldiers stood around us in the dark. Their weapons were tentatively relaxed, but I could sense their fingers were poised and ready to twitch. They continued to flank us as they led us from jungle, and the biggest of the men carried Stevo's huge, broken bulk over his shoulders as if my mate was nothing more than a sack of flour.

"My name is Sgt. Bodean Perry, but ya'll can call me Boots—or Sarge, if ya prefer," their commander informed us. He declined to introduce any of his men— nor did they present themselves.

Undeterred, Wog-Boy put out his hand for the shaking. "G'day, I'm Corporal Azzopardi," he made the introduction. "This is Lance Corporal Terence Pinfold, Private Angus MacKenna... and sleeping beauty over there is Private Steven Allowrie."

Boots ignored him and sniffed at the air. He wrinkled his nose in disgust, as if he'd detected something unpalatable. He shot me a look of repulsion before squinting derisively at Wog-Boy's outstretched hand.

He then snorted and spat out a wad of tobacco juice at the lad's feet. "Y'all aren't meant to be here." he dropped his voice to a low, serious tone, as he deliberately ignored Wog-Boy's hand and eyed our expressions.

Then, with a huge belly laugh, he grabbed Wog-Boy's hand and pumped it with aplomb. "I was just messin' wit' ya!" He guffawed. "Now let's get y'all inside an' git better acquainted!" He grinned, but the smile didn't quite reach his eyes.

Boots didn't even attempt to be subtle about

wiping the hand that just touched Wog-Boy's on his pants, and nobody else laughed along with him.

We walked on in silence. It must have been about a half an hour walk, yet I had to swallow down the myriad questions that swirled about my brain. Any opportunity I did take to speak elicited icy looks of murderous rage from Boots and his men, and I couldn't decide if we were being rescued by a bunch of miserable bastards or detained as an enemy.

A chill shiver shot down my spine as I wondered if the owner of the huge footprint we'd discovered would be any better company. Then my stomach lurched as I remembered poor Taz and Doc. I crashed into Macka's back as we were suddenly halted. Two of Boots' soldiers jogged on ahead, disappearing into the darkness and out of sight. The remaining four closed in around us, and I could feel their raw disdain and disgust towards us.

It worried me that, with all the thick bamboo groves around us, for all we knew, we could have just walked around in circles and still be in the middle of the jungle.

Fear spiked through my body at the thought—maybe Boots and his squad were leading us away from the base to spare themselves the hassle of disposing of our bodies. We walked on.

A few more steps, and the ground changed beneath my boots; after three months of patrolling in the jungle, you certainly notice a smooth, manmade surface under your feet.

This struck me as peculiar, because other than the trees uprooted by the creature, we were still surrounded by dense jungle.

It was then I noticed a soft light spilling onto the ground, and the two soldiers who had run on ahead busy opening up a thick, wide trapdoor in the jungle floor.

Chapter Four

Macka, Wog-Boy, and I shot each other a look.

We were all uneasy, but with the wall of M muscle and bullets around us, we didn't have any option but to follow the soldier's unspoken instructions as they pushed us forward toward the light.

Boots led the way, and his muscle came in from behind.

Despite his lifeless burden, the guy with Stevo on his shoulders climbed down into the darkness easier than any of us.

We must have climbed down at least twenty meters of metal ladder that was fixed to the wall of that concrete shaft, which grew darker and colder as we descended.

Finally at the bottom, we waited for the last man to hit the floor in a small, circular room that was thick with the damp stink of concrete and piss. A narrow metal door fitted within the curve of the room opened silently, and the bright, white light that shone from the hallway beyond temporarily blinded us.

"Let your eyes adjust, boys," Boots grunted. He and his team then wrenched our rifles from our hands and stripped us of ammo, grenades, and knives as easy as taking candy from a baby. We were pathetic; we didn't even resist.

The sick, cloying stench of ammonia was far stronger down here, yet the air was neither as damp nor stale as one would expect so far underground.

As my eyes began to adjust, I took in the sheer scale of the building we were ushered into— some kind of warehouse-sized underground bunker with a white, polished concrete floor. The space before us appeared to be set up as some kind of deployment point—there were soldiers' stretchers set up on the far side, along with head facilities and a small kitchen area. Next to that, a couple of men were sweating and grunting as they worked their already bunched muscles in a high-budget gym, which contained machines far more robotic than anything I'd ever seen before. And, towards the front of the place, there were several late model Jeeps and a few quad bikes parked up and facing a massive ramp.

In all, it was a stark contrast with where we'd spent the last few weeks and where we were expected to be.

Despite its familiarity to me as a military installation, the huge bunker seemed utterly alien, and I struggled to adjust—not only to the hard-white lights, but also to the surrealism of the place.

To our right was a huge double door. It was made from thick, riveted metal and was easily the size of the front of a barn. It had buzzing security lights and a small, metallic box to one side, which indicated swipe card access only.

As I watched, Boots and his team—bar one—made their way down to an armoury cage. With cool, mechanical efficiency, they unloaded and checked their hardware; they had weapons that were shiny, sophisticated, and definitely not anything I recognised.

They handed the weapons over the counter to a small, beefy-looking woman who handled them as if they were as light as paper planes.

I glanced briefly at the brute who Boots had left to watch over us. His weapon was held at that relaxed-yet-I'm-ready-to-pull-the-trigger angle in his arms. He observed us through squinting eyes, although he pretended not to. I studied him right back; the grunt's face looked to me like it had been chewed up and spat out by a Rottweiler. His skin was puckered and made shiny by countless scars, and his bulky body resembled that of a gnarled gorilla—his arms were almost as long and hairy as an ape's, and he had thick, black tufts of coarse hair curling up out of his collar and sleeves, the latter covering the backs of his hands like fuzzy gloves.

He caught me staring. "You got a problem, buddy?"

As he growled, he slapped his chewing tobacco around in his mouth; the sound reminded me of a seal clapping its fins to earn a herring or two. I watched as he clenched the muscles in his jaw, as if it was taking all his self-control not to reach out and snap my neck.

I glanced away from the guy—I'm no fuckin' hero.

Boots and his team each received a card on a lanyard in receipt of their weapons. They slung them around their thick, bulldog necks before circling us again.

Boots, with his jutting, exaggerated superhero jaw was also silvered with bristles and pockmarks. Similar to the Gorilla, his face resembled a Rotti's chew toy, and his expression was locked in a permanent snarl of contempt. It was then, in the unforgiving, bright light of the bunker, I noticed what appeared to be scars—or were they *scales*? Silver-white in colour, they ran up from under the collar of his shirt and disappeared into the pig-bristle of his stubble.

Despite the warmth, I shivered. In fact, our would-be rescuers were seriously the ugliest bunch of bastards I had ever seen. *No wonder the US hid these boys deep underground*, I mused.

Nonchalant, Boots swaggered his massive bulk past us, and on towards the double metal doors. He swiped his card down the keypad, and followed it with a press of his fat-headed thumb against a glowing panel. A smaller set of double doors—painted white to match the walls— adjacent to the larger ones swung open with a soft hiss. They'd blended into the wall so well that I hadn't even noticed them before.

Then, before we knew it, we were being

herded through the doors and down a short, white corridor as the small doors hissed shut behind us. The soldier with Stevo slung over his shoulder continued on straight ahead, while the rest of us were marshalled off to the right. We hovered inside a small room while Boots removed some test tubes from a little drawer.

"Blood sample, boys. For quarantine purposes," he said. He pricked each of our fingers and sealed the resulting droplets of blood into the tubes, which he marked with our initials and shoved into his pocket. He then herded us back out into the corridor.

Quarantining what? I thought, but the question never left my lips, as my brain was bustling with a million other questions. Boots, however, didn't look the sort to be handing out any answers.

The corridor opened up in another large area. This was made up of office cubicles, each one surrounded by glass panels. Polyester shirts, long hair, and well-rested faces told me the occupants of said cubicles were civilians—they all moved around in a frenzied buzz of activity. Here, the familiar smells of paper, coffee, and the rhythmic click of typewriters snapped me back to my pre-soldiering life as a cadet journalist—happier times. I chose Jenny, I chose wrong.

None of the civilians paid us any attention, or even acknowledged us—it was as if the boys and me simply didn't exist. But that's the punch line, right? There *we* were, in the middle of the jungle, fighting a war too many miles and years away from home, in a place where these office types, with their coffees, slacks, and sensible skirts simply shouldn't exist.

Boots buzzed us through yet another door, which opened into what could have been any other military dormitory: a large recreation area with a full bar, pool table, TV, books, and newspapers scattered around modern sofas—and with modern hippy music in the background. We were led through there, and along a corridor, where we were each deposited into an individual room and given simple instructions.

"You have thirty minutes for a shower, shit, and shave. There's a set of clothes at the end of your bed."

Boots said. The doors were then slammed shut and locked in our faces.

I walked around my room, which was barely bigger than a double back home. It housed a single bed with an empty desk and a metal chair. It had an unpleasantly *clinical* feel to it—far too white for a man who'd been living in the jungle, and too pure for a man who'd seen what I'd seen.

The narrow shower cubicle at the back of the room beckoned me, and I could not resist its siren call.

Tearing off my clothes, I recoiled at the foul stench of my own sour body odour—I honestly couldn't remember the last time I'd bathed. I stood in that hot shower for twenty of my allotted thirty minutes, letting the steaming water from the high-pressure head strip away layer after layer of blood, sweat, and grime.

Vigorously, I tried to scrub away the horrors of the last day with the minuscule square of carbolic soap, and I watched, mesmerized, as the trail of mud and gore slid down the plughole in a trail of grimy bubbles.

There was no mirror to shave by, just a shiny square of metal screwed to the wall. This, along with the steam from the shower and my incessant trembling, caused me to nick my face a good few times as I scratched away two days of growth. It felt good anyhow, despite the large, red rash that burned on my neck. Looking down at the bruises, scratches, and grazes—all at varying stages of healing—that covered most of my sun-deprived body, the shaving rash didn't seem all that out of place.

I was sliding into the oversized beige coveralls when I heard Boots' voice rumbling in the hall outside. I heard Macka reply something, and then a shout, a sharp cracking noise, then silence. My heart pounded hard in my chest as I threw on the white undershirt and crammed my socked feet into a pair of canvas lace-up sneakers that must have been about two sizes too big—I must've looked like a freaky-assed clown!

I'd felt safe for five minutes. All that evaporated when I heard the key slide into the lock and Boots turning the handle.

"Hurry up!" he barked. "I said *thirty minutes.* You've already had five bonus minutes, and still you can't get fucking dressed." Boots grunted at me and crinkled his nose in disgust.

"I haven't got a watch," I said. I showed him my wrists. "Where are the others?" As I fought to control my trembling hands, I fumbled with my shirt buttons.

"They've been... umm... *reassigned,*" Boots answered with a pensive look. "Yeah, they've been reassigned. Y'all see 'em later. Don't worry ya pretty lil head about 'em. We did manage to pull in your two buddies from the top of the hill, though. We'll be taking ya'll to 'em soon," he added. The fierce look he shot my way told me I shouldn't ask any more questions.

Boots led me through the office area, where I caught a few sidelong glances from the civilians; I was a tad relieved I wasn't invisible after all. I followed Boots down the corridor where I'd seen the soldier take Stevo—the sharp smell of antiseptic and the shiny white linoleum floors reminded me once more of a hospital.

Boots swiped his card and led me into a room with a row of hospital beds. Each one had thin, plastic curtains drawn around it, except for the last bed in the row.

There, I saw Stevo. He was all stretched out and had a petite Vietnamese nurse ministering to the myriad machines around his bed as they

65

beeped, whirred, and blinked.

"Is he going to be alright?" I asked as I tried to ignore Boots' massive hand on my shoulder as he pushed me on by. The nurse glanced up at me with a look of terror on her face. She pulled the curtains shut in a panic.

Boots' hand squeezed my shoulder—not too gently—and he guided me up to yet another small steel door.

This time, instead of swiping his card, he knocked.

The door opened with a soft hiss and Boots pushed me inside. The room was stark and bare, and was similar to the interview rooms I'd seen on cop shows. There was a stainless-steel table in the centre, which was bolted to the white floor and had two steel chairs on either side.

On one of the walls, a large glass mirror stretched the length of the room, and two little cameras clung to the corners near the ceiling.

I noticed all of this despite the stunning vision of the bombshell blonde who stood to attention next to the desk. Dressed in a grey skirt suit that hugged all the right curves, her gorgeous face stole most of my attention as her full lips pouted as she absently tapped a pencil against a pad of papers.

Glancing up with ice blue eyes, a polite smile flashed upon the young woman's face as she motioned for me to sit down. "Lance Corporal Terence Pinfold, Bravo Platoon, 11/28th

66

Battalion," she stated.

"Umm, yes, Ma'am," I mumbled back. I was not sure if I was actually meant to answer her or not.

She stared into my eyes, and smiled with real warmth. And for the first time since being forced into the place, I relaxed and felt a little more comfortable.

However, I did sense an icy edge to this beautiful vixen, and I was not entirely ready to be charmed.

"Oh please, I'm sorry—my name is Dr. Jacinta Harding. I work for the US Government, and I specialise in biogenetics and psychiatric research. You and your men stumbled upon us here, and now we're in the difficult position as to what to do about it." I couldn't place the woman's accent, but in all honesty, I didn't damn care. With those legs, she could have sounded like a squawking chicken and she'd still be sexy as all hell.

I shrugged my shoulders. I had already assumed as much—well at least as much as the place was some US

Government Black Op. Just what biogenetics and psychiatric research had to do with it, I really didn't want to know.

"With all due respect, Dr. Harding, if knowledge makes me more of a liability, I don't care to know anything more. If you understand what I mean, Ma'am."

"Yes, of course, Lance Corporal Pinfold."

"Pinny. Please, Ma'am, just call me Pinny."

"Are you of Aboriginal descent, Pinny? *Australian* Aboriginal?" She smiled at me.

I shrugged my shoulders. "Does it matter?"

I didn't tick the box on my enlistment forms as identifying as Aboriginal simply because A) I didn't think it mattered and B) It's none of their fucking business.

Harding looked me up and down in a way that chilled me to my bones. "It always matters, Pinny."

"Told you he was a nigga. You can smell it." Boots grunted. I jerked upright; I've been called that name plenty of times before, and he could call me all the names in the world, but I doubt he'd come up with something I hadn't heard before. Other than his dog-ugly looks, Boots didn't strike me as a man of great originality.

I shrugged my shoulders and relaxed back into the chair; the redneck bastard just wasn't worth an effort. I chanced a quick glance at Harding, and I saw her ice blue eyes narrow as she glared at Boots. Boots had straightened himself up ramrod tall and clenched his fists into tight balls—I'd been in enough brawls to know he would take me in a wink, but it might just be worth it.

"Gentlemen, please." Harding drew all attention back to herself as she sat on the desk. Her sweet-smelling perfume tickled my olfactories, and my eyes feasted upon those long, slender legs that flashed hypnotically from beneath that oh-so tight skirt. She reminded me of a cobra uncoiling slowly to lull me into a dulled state of mind so I'd not see the strike coming. And, by God, it was working. To be fair, though, I'd seen very few women in the weeks previous—especially not one as beautiful as this.

Dr. Harding twisted her torso around to look directly at me, which pushed her more than generous breasts in my direction. Her shirt pulled taut across those delectable mounds of soft flesh, and as close as I was, I couldn't miss the delicate pattern of the lace bra underneath, nor the shadows of large, dark nipples that seemed to extend under my gaze, beckoning me. I smelled her sweet flesh beneath the perfume now, and my throat dried. *Was she trying to seduce me?* I wondered.

I squirmed uncomfortably in my seat as I couldn't ignore the increasing weight in my groin, which was noticeable despite my baggy coveralls. Cold and calculating, Harding's eyes flashed up and down my body.

Then she smiled at Boots and slid off the desk.

"Hmmm... you're a hard man to read, Pinny. I want you to work for us, or should I say work *with* us? What do you think, Boots, darling? He would be a *perfect* fit for the team," she all but purred.

Boots gritted his teeth in response. He wore a bitter smile on his ugly-bastard face.

69

"Work? Doing what? I already have a job," I answered.

Harding smiled. "As far as the Australian Government is concerned, you are no longer... available for employment," she told me. "Boots, can you please bring me the case?"

Boots grunted and picked up one of three steel cases on the floor. He laid it on the small desk in front of Harding and then returned to his corner.

"Good boy," I teased, as if talking to an obedient dog.

Boots' face tightened, and I felt the rage flowing from him.

A single look from Harding backed him down.

The doctor clicked open the case. Inside it, there were a handful of canisters and syringes. I recoiled at the syringe part—I hated needles. Snapping on a pair of rubber gloves, Harding's eyes flickered over me with a look not unlike a butcher assessing a cow for the slaughterhouse.

"Wait, what exactly do you mean?" I blurted out. "*No longer available for employment?* " I asked with a lump in my throat.

"Lance Corporal Pinfold... sorry, *Pinny,* I just need to fit some equipment on you, so we can run some tests."

"Umm, no, you're not. You need my permission *and* my country's permission, and you do not have either." I surprised myself by my bravado; as I said, I hated needles.

"You're in my lab, honey, and your country has already listed you as KIA—thanks to the report we sent them." Harding smiled and my stomach dropped. She could have been bluffing, but I wasn't going to volunteer myself—not for a fucking needle. Her eyes flickered with impatience. "I really don't want to do this the hard way. I want you to work with us, Pinny. We're doing valuable, ground-breaking research here; not just for national security, but for *global* security as well."

"I already have a job, thank you," I insisted.

"No." Harding was firm. "As I've already explained, that role has been terminated. Besides, that's well below your qualifications. The *real* war is coming, and you can help us win it. Wouldn't you like to work under me?"

Her smile was most suggestive. I looked away to draw in a long breath, and saw Boots blanch at Harding's comment.

"I really just want to go home."

"Go home? To Jenny? Didn't you run away from home—isn't that why you are here?"

My heart sunk into my guts at the sound of her name.

"What the fuck do you know about Jenny?"

"I know enough. Our intelligence system is beyond anything you can comprehend, Pinny. We even know where she lives."

"Bullshit."

"Number 10…"

What the hell?!

"Leave Jenny the fuck out of this."

"Oh, I want to. But that is not up to me. That's totally your decision."

"Is this what you call *working with you*, manipulating me by threatening my girl? Fuck that for a joke." I winced—Jenny wasn't *my girl* anymore.

"I don't want to do this the hard way. You're far too valuable not to have on the team. Let us sort you out, and I'll gladly show you what we've been doing here.

You can be the answer to my dreams *and* keep Jenny and your son safe." She leaned in close.

"My son? I think your intel is faulty."

"Maybe," she purred, "but the boy is more likely yours. Don't you want to keep him safe?"

I froze, my heart pounding in my chest. The maths worked out—I already knew that much. Jenny said he wasn't mine, and had always insisted he was Simon's—she didn't want me to be the baby's father regardless of who's DNA he had. But how the fuck did Harding know any of this? I glanced at her cool, calculating eyes.

Manipulative bitch.

"Yeah, thanks, but no thanks, Doc."

"Boots, can you secure Pinny please? Hopefully he will soon see reason."

"It would be my pleasure, Ma'am," the big grunt drawled as he lumbered over towards me. Jumping to my feet, I knocked the chair over, and its metallic clang echoed about the room as Harding watched on in mild amusement.

Boots was at least an entire foot taller and easily an extra fifty kilos of solid muscle than me, so I knew I wasn't going to take a hit and stay standing. My boxing days at the YMCA—Dad's idea of self-defence—allowed me to duck his first attack. However, a sudden unexpected jerk on my shirt collar almost lifted me off my feet...

So shocked with Harding's strength, I moved too late, and Boots' swinging hook glanced off my jaw.

The force of the punch spun me around on my feet and I fell over my own tangle of legs. Boots' bear-like grip almost crushed my shoulder as he pulled me back to my feet. He reached back and launched from short range, and as my head snapped back, I descended into blackness.

Chapter Five

My jaw throbbed like all hell when I woke up. I found myself laid out on a hospital gurney M with sticky sweat trickling down my back.

"Hey, Pinny... you awake yet, mate?" I snapped my head around to my left, which had the room spinning. I saw Chook sitting up in the bed across from me.

"Mate, it's good to see you," I mumbled. My numb jaw refused to cooperate, yet genuine pleasure warmed me to see the young man was still alive. I then remembered where we were, and fancied his odds a whole lot more out there in the jungle.

"Pinny, oh boy, am I glad to see you?! What's that on your head? These blokes scared the hell out of us. I was all set to keep sitting right there until they said Wog-Boy had sent them. Where *is* Wog-Boy?" he rattled on and his pimply face broke into a huge smile—that kinda broke my heart.

Something was tight wrapped around my head, which felt as if I was wearing a hat three sizes too small. I examined my throbbing skull with my hand.

My fingers rasped against the prickle of shaven hair.

They'd shaved my entire head!

Assholes!

It wasn't too hard to find the metal band. It was wrapped tight around the back of my skull from ear to ear. I pulled on it to try and remove it, only to wince when I discovered it was secured to my skull. Slick with sweat, my fingers trembled when I discovered the screws on the otherwise smooth band. The bastards had actually *screwed* the thing to my fucking skull!

I froze when my fingers touched wires that trailed down the back of my neck. *What the hell?* I thought as I continued tracing them until they disappeared into the flesh at the top of my neck.

Taking in several deep breaths, holding and releasing to the count of five, I tried to calm myself before panic took over. I'd once dated this hippy chick who'd told me all about yoga and breathing stuff. I don't remember much, except if you calm your breathing, you can calm yourself. It didn't help too much, but it was just enough.

My head still spinning, I searched around the room.

There were four beds, hospital gurneys, and nothing else. A body, curled up tight, hid under the bed on the far side of Chook. I pointed and mouthed *Snowy?* Chook nodded, looking glum, and opened his mouth. I silenced him with a finger to my lips—I didn't want to disturb Snowy any more than need be; I didn't want to have to cope with his hysteria.

"I dunno where Wog-Boy is. We were sent to

separate rooms for a shower, and I haven't seen him or Macka since. Stevo took a hard hit to the head, it looks like they're looking after him." My jaw ached as I spoke.

"Doc?" Chook asked. I think he already knew the answer. He dropped his head when I shook mine. Poor Doc, torn open like a sardine can and propped up like some cheap sidewalk art exhibition. I was at least glad Chook hadn't seen that fucking mess.

"Where are we, Pinny? I don't think these guys are regular US Army."

"Dunno, Chook. There's nothing regular about this place. There's a woman scientist... she's one fine piece of ass, but an absolute nutter, if you ask me."

"Harding? You met her, too?" Chook blushed. "I think she seemed... umm... ok," he squeaked. I smiled at him. Poor kid. One day he'll learn the prettier they come, the crazier they are. It's just another one of God's cruel jokes on us blokes. Harding is not just regular crazy, she's clearly seriously bat-shit crazy; I'm surprised Chook came out of that meeting alive.

"Watch her, mate. She's gone tropo— absolutely bloody crazy." I wriggled myself up in the bed. I was just pondering the notion of getting out of it when I heard a *click* and *whoosh* of the door, and I snatched my leg back under the sheets.

Boots' mangy leer came through the door first,

followed by Harding—who was now wearing a snug lab coat that accentuated her hour-glass figure to perfection—and two other henchmen. I pushed myself tight against the bedhead as they walked straight past me and headed direct to Snowy's bed.

"What the hell is this shit you've put in my head?" I demanded to know. Harding was so intent and focused on Snowy that I don't think she even registered me—if she had, she chose to ignore my question. Boots pinned me to the bed with an aggressive look as one of his goons—the short squat one—stepped back towards me; his black, beady eyes told me he'd just *love* any excuse to tear me limb from limb.

"It's just a monitoring device," Harding said over her shoulder. "Mason, can you please check it's working for me?"

"Monitoring *what*, exactly?" I received no answer.

Mason looked like a small stack of bricks: square, squat, and packed with power. He pulled out a metal rod from his pocket and scanned it over my head.

He smirked as I flinched in anticipation of him hitting me about the head with it. Instead, he just waved it over me until he heard a series of beeps and a bunch of lights flashed. "All good, Doctor Harding," he grunted.

"Why doesn't Chook have one?" I asked. I was annoyed at myself for flinching.

"We have different plans for Mr. Jacobs," Harding said as she paused by at Chook's bedside and dropped a bomb of a smile on the lad.

"Hello, Doctor Harding." Chook's face flushed in crimson.

"Hello, Mr. Jacobs," she purred.

"Raymond. Please, Doctor Harding, just *Raymond*,"

Chook wheezed. I saw the kid starting to hyperventilate and nervously wipe his clammy hands on the bed sheets.

The whole room permeated with the reek of sex, warm flesh, and soft sweat. Even *my* throat went dry.

"I can't believe you're just eighteen, Raymond. They must mature young where you're from." She playfully squeezed his paltry bicep.

"Liverpool, Sydney, Doctor."

"Liverpool? Sydney? I heard it's most divine there."

She gazed at poor Chook like he was a God. Damn, she was good. She was also a blatant liar—everyone knows Liverpool is a total shithole.

"Ur, yeah, well I guess it's alright."

"Oh, yes, of course. Well, Mr. Jacobs—sorry, I mean Raymond—if you could give me a few moments with Mr. White here, then I'll give you some personal attention." Harding smiled with promise in her eyes and walked her fingers up his arm. And when she cupped his cheek in her hand, I'm not sure if Chook came or pissed his pants—it was quite possibly both.

I caught Boots' eyes as he stood there in the corner closest to Snowy's bed. Other than him being a racist bastard, I couldn't begin to understand why the man hated me so. Nonetheless, it was an energy unto itself, and I could actually feel it pulsing through the room. I watched as Harding opened that familiar briefcase and placed it onto a small, steel table one of her minions had brought in with him.

"What are you doing with my mate?" I asked her.

"He's not been well—a touch of shellshock, I think."

Harding glanced over at me while writing something on a clipboard. "Oh, I'm well aware of that, Terence.

We have the medicine to, well, *help* him with that condition. Although his adrenalin levels are long burnt out, I'm expecting our formula will give us the result we want. However, there are always contra-indications, risks to any medical procedure..."

"*Medicine*? What medicine? I think it best if you just get us back to our own people. They'll take care of him." I began to raise myself from the bed. It was only then I noticed I was in one of those awful papery hospital gowns that gape open at the back to give the world a free view of my ass.

By the time I'd stood up and pulled it closed tight around my butt, Mason—the short goon—had returned to my bedside and pushed me back down onto the bed with his massive paw. "I'm going to have to ask you to remain in your bed," the goon growled through chipped teeth.

I hesitated for a moment, as any sane man would, but when I saw Harding leaning over Snowy and then draw down green liquid into a syringe, I pushed forward.

"She's a Doctor, Pinny, I'm sure she knows what she's doing," Chook stammered.

"What kind of bloody Doctor, Chook? What kind of a Doctor hides below ground in the middle of fucking war zone, and surrounded by ugly bastards? No *normal* Doctor, that's for sure." I dropped my hospital gown and used both hands to get past the solid rock of Boots' goon.

It just wasn't going to happen.

No matter how hard I shoved, the guy didn't waver an inch. It was then I caught sight of the inside of my arm, and saw the trail of needle marks in my dusky skin.

"What the fuck is this shit?" I pointed at my arm in disgust.

I forgot all about it, though, the moment that needle went into Snowy.

He sat bolt-upright just seconds after Harding withdrew the needle. His skin appeared translucent as his veins turned black beneath his skin. His jaw distended and locked open in agony. I froze as Chook's protest faded into nothing and Boots' other goon—equally as hideous as the first, yet taller and leaner—stepped closer to Chook's bed.

Snowy's hands curled into half-clutching fists as he rubbed and scratched at his body, which began to blister.

Within seconds, his scratching was uncontrollable, and poor Snowy raked his nails down his face to tear his flesh into jagged, oozing wounds which bled pitch-black blood. I tried my best to get over to him, but the goon held me at bay as if I was little more than a scrap of a child.

Chook froze in shock.

Snowy's body began jerking in violent spasms, his jaw un-locked—snapping down—and he bit off the tip of his tongue. Blood, black as ink, splashed everywhere as Boots rushed in to restrain him. I noticed Harding, her eyes glistening with lust, as she wiped away a droplet of blood and brought it to her lips.

"You, sick, fucking, vampire bitch! *Get away from my mate!* " I shouted, much to the doctor's amusement.

Boots restrained Snowy with the straps installed beneath the mattress. The bed jerked and rattled as Snowy erupted into wave upon wave of spasms. Having experienced a childhood of Aussie Rules football, I quickly recognised the all-too-familiar pop of joints dislocating and tendons snapping.

Snowy's moans of pains were muffled by a cloth Harding shoved in his mouth to stem the bleeding from his lacerated tongue.

Mason smiled and stepped aside to allow me to run to Snowy's side. Scrambling out of bed to join me, Chook clutched tight to hold his hospital gown around his pimply ass and looked all self-conscious at Harding.

Harding leaned over Snowy with a metal rod in her hand. It let off a series of high-pitched pings before she passed it off to Boots and scribbled away on her clipboard.

I moved to elbow her aside, but she neatly dodged me. I undid Snowy's restraints and his head lolled to the side and his eyes were clamped shut. His cheeks were puffed out with bloodied gauze, which I didn't dare remove.

Anger began the slow burn in my belly. "What the hell did you do to him, you sick bitch? We're part of the Australian Army, and you can't... you just can't do this goddam shit to us!" My anger killed any sense of caution.

"You're *dead*, remember? MIA at best," the doctor reminded me. "Your people have already forgotten about you, Pinny. And, please, move out of my way, before I ask Boots to assist you."

Gingerly rubbing at my jaw, I stepped around Harding and made my way back to the other side of Snowy to sit on Chook's bed. I caught Chook's eye and with my finger circling next to my ear I whispered,

"Tropo, mate."

Chook's eyes were wide with fear, and seeing Snowy seemed beyond immediate help, he slunk back into his bed. He was as terrified as me, and there was nothing I could say or do for the kid; I noticed he was trembling.

Bloody hell.

"So, Mr. Jacobs—I mean *Raymond*. It's your turn now." Harding grinned as Chook blanched, and it wasn't from youthful lust this time.

"I'm feeling just fine now, Dr. Harding. In fact, I think I might take a nap instead," he said.

"A nap?" Harding laughed. "I'm quite certain a virile young man like you doesn't need a *nap,* " she mocked as Chook floundered for words.

"Leave the kid alone, Harding," I snapped. "We're not here to play your games. Just leave him alone. Let him go back home—he's not going to say anything, and even if he did, no one would believe him anyway. He's just a kid."

Harding stared at me. Anger flickered beyond those ice blue eyes, and I didn't like it one little bit. But then it was gone.

After a long, dramatic sigh, Harding reached up and removed her golden tresses from her tight bun. Arching her back and pushing out those delectable mounds, she tossed her golden mane around and regarded Chook coquettishly. It was so bloody cliché, so like every porn movie I'd ever sat through with tented trousers, I had to stifle a laugh.

Her eyes flicked across at me, dangerous and violent, and I saw she held poor Chook like putty in her hand.

He was hypnotised. Poor bastard was going to die a virgin, cherry un-popped—it just wasn't fair.

Harding slunk over to his bedside. She ran her hands up along his leg and Chook quivered like a rabbit in the headlights. He knew he was being hunted, but there wasn't a damn thing he could do about it. His jaw popped open and bobbed up and down as he tried to summon words, *any* words.

"You're not a kid, are you Raymond?"

"No Ma'am, I'm *eighteen* this summer." Chook wheezed and a glistening film of sweat broke out on his forehead.

"Do you want me to make you a man, Raymond?"

Harding purred.

"Well, I *am* a man, technically. Already." Chook gulped and flinched from her touch.

"Leave him alone, Harding," I interrupted. It was useless—Boots and his goons were closing in on me.

Poor Chook was about to be devoured.

"Be quiet, Terence, this is your final warning. I will get to you in due course," the doctor hissed. She nodded to Boots to pass her another metal case. Boots did so and then grabbed Chook's shoulders and pushed him down into the mattress.

"Please don't do this," Chook begged. "You don't *need* to do this."

"Oh, but I do. It's your gift to yourself, to me, to us,"

Harding cooed.

Angry with frustration, I stood up. I hate seeing people being bullied, most likely because I'd been on the receiving end my entire life. I could see the fucking game Harding was playing, and poor Chook needed someone to stand up for him.

"He's just a kid, dammit!" I managed to shout, just before the tall, skinny goon picked me up by the neck and pushed me face down onto my bed.

A cold breeze caressed my ass as my gown flew open and the goon did a long slow whistle. "I wouldn't mind a piece of this when you're done with him, Doc," he said. The goon then laid his weight across my shoulders with one arm and he felt twice as heavy as he should have. Then the sick bastard started caressing my backside.

"Get the fuck off me!" I screamed as I bucked, trying to dislodge him. The bastard just laughed and grabbed my ass cheek, bruising it in a vice-like grip. The blunt end of one fingertip prodded itself against my puckered ring, and I whimpered with the pain and humiliation of it.

"Don't worry, Pinny, I'll be right," Chook tried to reassure me. "Please, Doc, get your man off him, he isn't going to bother you anymore—I promise. Right, Pinny?" I couldn't see what was happening, but the fucker released my ass cheek and removed his concrete weight off my back.

"You are *so* mine, baby. My name is Johnny, you'll be screaming it later," the tall goon whispered with stinking garlic breath in my ear. My stomach churned, my ass puckered, and goose bumps flared across my body.

He pulled me back off the bed and wrapped his arm around my chest to pin my arms down and pull me hard against his body. "Keep wriggling, I'll enjoy it more than you," he promised, and rubbed the bulge of his crotch against my lower back.

Harding drew back on the syringe and aimed it down towards Chook's arm...

Snowy sat bolt upright in his bed and, roaring in anger and pain, he ripped the gauze out of his mouth.

Everybody jumped.

Throwing himself off the bed, Snowy launched himself at Harding with teeth bared and coated with tar-black blood. I heard the syringe shatter on the floor, and Harding curse under her breath. Snowy's eyes rolled back in his head, and thin ribbons of blood ran down his torn cheeks.

Boots reacted in an instant, and put himself between Snowy and Harding. Snowy didn't make it far, before his body jerked and contorted mid-step, yellowish liquid ran from his ears and nose, and he tore at his face.

Veins, twisted like black tree roots, ruptured, and I watched on helplessly as sickly blue-black flowers bloomed under my friend's skin over the entirety of his body. The petals crumbled and shrunk into a grey ash, as Snowy made one more step towards Harding before collapsing lifeless on the floor.

"What a shame, he was a handsome one," said Harding. "Boots, can you get your boys to remove this... *thing*?" She pointed at Snowy with one white patent pump.

"What the hell is that shit?! What have you done to my mate?!" I shouted, and tried hard to breathe against the crushing restraint that was the goon's arm. Chook sat bolt upright in bed, arms and legs wrapped around himself, eyes wide, and jaw dropped open in shock. He flinched from Harding's touch as she tried to caress his cheek.

"I'm sorry, Raymond. I'll just have to get your friend here sorted, and then I can come back and spend some special time with you."

"What...what are you going to do with him?" Chook stuttered. Harding wrinkled her nose and poked at the Snowy's prone body again with her foot.

"Well, I'll have to autopsy him to find out what went wrong—and then dispose of him. But don't let that bother you, Raymond. I want you to stay here, relax, and enjoy your time." She leaned in close, her lips all puffed and pouty. "I want you to think about what we can get up to together." She then turned to look at me. "Next time we'll be alone. Terence is a real party pooper, isn't he? I think he's jealous, is all," she giggled.

Chapter Six

Chook slumped in his bed.

"They are going to kill us, aren't they, Pinny?" he asked for the hundredth time.

"There are some things worse than dying, mate," I answered grimly for the hundredth time. I explored the band on my head, and wondered what the hell we were in for. My brain buzzed as I tried to piece the puzzle together—I just couldn't see any way out of this. We knew too much of nothing, but it was still too much. *But why not just kill us outright, up there in the jungle?* My head started to pound with a cycle of thought that quickly became a twenty-car pile-up—with no fucking survivors.

I don't know how much longer it was before we heard the *click* and *whoosh* of the door. Boots barged in and threw a stack of clothes in my direction. "Get dressed. Harding wants you."

"And me?" asked Chook, his voice unsteady.

"Ya'll are gonna stay here for a while. Have that nap you wanted not long ago," said Boots. Chook paled even more.

"She'll be right, mate. I'll be back soon," I said to Chook as I shoved myself into the clothes. Chook just looked at me with those colossal puppy dog, blue eyes, which implored me not to go, not to leave him alone. I glanced at Boots. I really didn't have a choice.

We didn't have to walk far through the twist and turn of corridors before we hit a junction point. There, the blonde she-devil in a lab coat, Harding, waited with a wide grin on her full lips.

"Look, Doc, do what you want with me. Just, please, I'm begging you. Let the kid go. Give him a chance," I begged.

Her eyes opened wide with delight. "What a great idea," she said with a grin. She beckoned Boots over and whispered in his ear loud enough for me to hear, giggling as an excited schoolgirl with juicy gossip. "I know it's unusual, but it's a viable option. Let's give young Mr. Jacobs a fighting chance. What do you say, Boots?"

Unhappy, Boots grunted, rolled his shoulders, cracked his neck, and stomped off down the corridor.

"Don't worry," Harding chirped, "he'll be back in a moment. You are correct, Terence, all men deserve a chance, and I think we might just make an exception to our strict rules for your friend, Mr. Jacobs."

I didn't trust the woman as far as I could throw her, and I had the feeling I'd just fallen into a trap—or pushed Chook into one. I just nodded without enthusiasm and I wished I'd kept my mouth shut.

Reaching into the pocket of her lab coat, Harding removed the metal rod Mason had scanned over me earlier. She stepped in close. I shuddered involuntarily and tried to step away, only to find the wall behind me.

Harding smiled a sweet, sexy smile that on any other day, in any other place, would have melted me. Instead, it felt predatory—animal, even, and I just couldn't shake the sensation she wanted to eat me.

"It's okay, Terence, I'm just going to get some baseline readings," she explained. "This band monitors your heart rate, pulse, nervous system, and various readings from your brain."

"Why?" Shut your mouth, Pinny! I screamed inwardly at myself. You don't want to know!

"It lets us know when to give you your next dose of... *medication*." She waved the metal rod around in the air.

"Why?" Shut the fuck up, Pinny!

"We measure the optimum adrenalin levels that will enable our formula to adhere to your DNA better. It helps prevent unfortunate incidences like with your friend, Snowy. I mean, his chances were always slim, but we salvage what we can. Ultimately, it's to help you become better soldiers."

"I don't want to be a better soldier. I just want to get home in one piece."

"Well, maybe you need to be a better soldier, so you can *have* a home and a family in one piece." She put a hand on my shoulder. I swallowed my disgust.

"What do you mean by that...?" Curiosity got

91

the better of me once again.

Before she could answer, Boots stomped back around the corner, glowering as he saw Harding's hand resting on my shoulder. "It's organised," he growled.

"Excellent. Come this way, Terence," Harding commanded as she spun around on her heel and swiped us into a long narrow room, which was actually more of a hallway or galley. It sported a large glass window that ran its entire length.

I gasped out loud. Looking through the window, I saw Wog-Boy relaxing on a bed. Dr. Harding nodded at Boots, and he pulled at a lever that stuck out from the wall.

"Do you believe in aliens, Pinny?" Harding's steel-blue eyes studied my comrade with excitement.

"There are stories from our ancestors, from what we call the *Dreamtime*— our *Genesis,* as you will. Well, some have been interpreted as run-ins with UFOs.

I'd heard of UFO sightings, of course, my Mother's people speak of it often. It is far more common in the North, up near the Territory, or out at Uluru. But as far as they're concerned, they're a white fella's problem."

"No blackfella has been abducted yet," I told Harding with a grin.

"Oh, good. This will make it easier for you to process then."

I followed her gaze and spotted a ripple of

light at the door that led into Wog-Boy's room. At first, I thought I saw a shadow, but then it flickered and formed into a beautiful woman. Stark naked and exquisite, she looked as if she'd just stepped straight out of a men's magazine.

Wog-Boy's eyes darted towards her, and grew large in confusion.

"Who is she?" I demanded as I watched the stunning young woman stroll over to Wog-Boy and sit on the end of his bed.

"Who is she? She's Betty, and she is our breeder.

Betty is an alien." Harding replied as nonchalantly as if commenting upon the weather. Not once did she take her eyes away from Betty's seduction of my helpless comrade.

"An alien? As in an *illegal* alien?" I half-joked.

"No. As in the extra-terrestrial variety," Dr. Harding responded. She shot me a glance as if she found me to be intolerably stupid. "Betty is from a planet named *Carfete*. She was a refugee—for lack of a better word."

"If they're all so beautiful, what have we been so scared of all these years?" I laughed as nervousness twisted my guts, and I tried not to watch Wog-Boy in what should be a private moment.

Harding explained with a distinctly unprofessional, lascivious tone to her silky-smooth voice, "Oh, that isn't Betty's natural appearance. She takes the form of whatever is in your mind's eye as the perfect mate. It's in her genetic makeup to look irresistible—so your instinct to breed is driven as strongly as her own. Watch as she works her magic on Corporal Azzopardi. We can never study this enough."

"I don't feel comfortable watching my boss getting his rocks off. So, if this is what you perverted scientists like to do for kicks, you go for it. Can I please leave?" I still couldn't stop myself ogling as the nude woman kissed Wog-Boy's neck and sensuously massaged his shoulders, her full, pert breasts brushing against the clean bandages of his face. There's just something about death and trauma that has people slowing down at car accidents and gazing into coffins at funerals—sex is much the same. That's the best excuse I have, anyway.

"Just a few more minutes, Pinny. This is the best way for any man to finish, wouldn't you agree, Boots?

Unfortunately, Corporal Azzopardi posesses, like most Europeans, impure DNA. Which means, sadly, this is the best role for him at our facility. At least he is fulfilling all his fantasies before he... plays his role in our trial." She giggled and Boots grunted.

"Just what exactly did you mean by *breeder*?" I asked, desperate to distract myself from the impromptu sex show that was taking place; Betty was busy disrobing the fully consenting, enamoured Wog-Boy.

"Corporal Azzopardi is going to donate his semen, so Betty can give us more alien/human hybrids for testing and projects," Dr. Harding explained. Her attention was captivated by what was going on at the other side of the glass. "But he must be at a certain level of arousal for the optimal extraction to occur—which is Betty's job."

I watched on, helpless, as Betty the freakin' Alien mounted Wog-Boy and rode him hard. His back arched to meet her body and his face clenched in bliss. *How much more arousal does one man need?* I asked myself.

And what do they mean by hybrid babies?

I was about to open my mouth to ask Dr. Harding when she interrupted. "Now, now, *now*," she purred as she stared through the thick glass of the window. Her voice was thick with her own arousal, as if she was the one naked and fucking my section leader with such wanton abandon.

Betty's face, contorted with pleasure, flickered into a mottled grey colour, and her eyes grew extraordinarily large. Her nose flared wide as she slammed herself down hard on Wog-Boy's body, and Wog-Boy's expression changed from orgasmic bliss to agonising terror as a thick jet of blood squirted out from between their thighs.

Betty convulsed with what appeared to be pleasure, and in an instant, she transformed into a grotesque reptilian creature. All pretence of human form was discarded, and she stood up on two clawed feet. Her skin was now a mottled, scaly grey, and those magnificent breasts were no longer on her chest. Large grey cords—fleshy dreadlocks—hung from her head like so many dormant snakes.

Done with her wild breeding, Betty slid off Wog-Boy's lap. He, for his part, writhed in agony and clutched at his crotch—from where an alarming amount of blood was flowing. Betty sat herself down next to the bed and bent over to lick her thighs clean—much like a pet cat. Except, her tongue was long and forked like a snake's.

My mind spun and my guts churned at what I'd just witnessed. I just couldn't help but stare at the raw, exposed grotesquery of the alien's sex, as between her blood-drenched legs, instead of the soft, fleshy flower of a vagina, there gaped a vicious maw which was ringed with row upon row of sharp, inward-curving teeth. From where I was standing, the hideous thing appeared to be smiling at me!

My jaw dropped open in horror and my eyes darted to Wog-Boy. He was bleeding profusely from the torn, ragged flesh where his dick had been. Rolling on the floor in agony, he curled in a ball as far away as possible from the disgusting creature that had mutilated him. His face was contorted in pain as he shrieked, but the thick glass muffled his cries.

I hammered hard on the window with the palm of my hand, but it didn't even budge. There was nothing I could do to help my comrade, and my helplessness rolled into raw anger.

"Jesus, Mary, Mother of Christ! What the fuck happened to him?!" I roared at Harding. I pushed her up hard against the glass. Feeling the warmth of her body and the laboured rise and fall of her firm breasts, I paid little attention to the insistent beeps of the band around my head.

In an instant, Boots slammed me with brute force into the back wall. Dr. Harding straightened her lab coat and composed herself. Winded or not, I was still full of rage.

"You're sick! This is all sick! You need to be bloody shot!" I grunted in short, breathless spurts.

"It's just how they breed—with humans, anyway,"

Harding was quite matter of fact about the whole thing.

She ran her metal rod around the band on my head, and it began beeping and whistling. "Interesting." She sounded distracted. "We tried for years with artificial insemination, but it never took. The alien's bodies need to consume a human males' entire sex organ for impregnation to occur. They actually suck the testicles out right through the penis. It really is absolutely *fascinating.*"

My legs cramped up and wobbled underneath me. A group of lab-coated staff ran into the room beyond the observation window. One pushed

Betty into a corner with a long, metal pole while the others attended to Wog-Boy. Distracted, I didn't even feel the bite of the needle as it entered my arm—it was the sensation of iced razor blades sliding through my system, along with Boots' pincer grip on my shoulder, that roused me.

"Don't worry, they survive. Most of the time," Dr.

Harding said, as if that somehow negated the fact that my commanding officer had just had his dick and balls ripped off. "Let's go, Pinny, I think our next test should be ready." She pulled my hand into hers and dragged me towards the exit.

Just as we were leaving, I saw Betty flicker back from her vile alien form and into a tall Negro woman with skin the colour of sun-kissed onyx. The man pinning her to the corner relaxed, and then they were all out of view.

Chapter Seven

My head spun wildly. I stumbled around with the woozy sensation of being drunk.

"What was in that needle?"

"Just something to help you become the best you can be." Harding smiled. I cringed at the touch of her powder-soft hand as she grabbed mine to support me; it rubbed smooth and sensual against my rough fingers, and yet never had I been more repulsed by a woman. Her nails may have been shiny and perfectly manicured, but her hands were tainted by blood and pain. In my daze, I thought they had taken on a greyish hue under the florescent lights—must have been the drugs.

I snatched my hand away. Right then, I would have much preferred to be holding a giant, maggot-infested turd than the Doctor's hand. Boots hissed at me, but Dr.

Harding just waved him off as they walked me out and down the small corridor. She turned to me and asked,

"Why do you think the United States is so interested in Vietnam, Pinny?"

"I don't want to know," I answered as the room still spun around me "Oh, Jesus, what *have* you given me?"

"Well," Harding continued, "this war has

nothing to do with communism, that's for sure. Communism, *liberalism*, is merely a perfect misdirection that feeds directly on the fear of ignorant Americans. It's really all about aliens."

"Aliens?" I gulped. My head was fogged up with confusion and shock—I prayed I was stuck in a bad dream. "You let that fucking thing do that... to my mate. You're a sick bitch."

"Someone has to get their hands dirty." Harding sighed as if she was speaking to a troublesome child.

"You see, Americans can handle communism—they believe they can fight ideological warfare with guns and helicopters; if you kill enough of the opposing point of view, you take the danger out of it. But, if the general population knew aliens existed, they'd just panic.

Humans know they can't compete physically or intellectually with a superior culture, which is why they have people like *us* to prepare the world and to protect mankind against them," Dr. Harding explained as she swiped her card to open up a sizeable, double-steel door.

"Back in 1952, the CIA and the NSC-4 tracked a ship that landed near here in South Vietnam. It was one of the first ships reported in which there were survivors.

We had to race against the Russians, China, North *and* South Vietnam to claim it. Luckily, we already had agents in Korea.

"The South Vietnamese still beat America and

the North to the ship, but couldn't hold on to it unless they accepted our help and conditions. We moved the entire facility forty kilometres south from the original crash site and put everything underground to keep it away from the competition. And, since there was no way we could send enough American troops into the area without a valid reason, some smart cookie in the Pentagon came up with the whole war-on-communism ruse. We simply set the trap and let the North fall into it. War is always a sure-fire way to launder money out of the American taxpayers, anyway."

"Why are you telling me all this, Doc? I don't give a shit. I just wanna get my mates and go home."

"You're a valuable resource, Pinny. I want you on our team—to understand the bigger picture, just as Boots does. Your DNA responds very well to alien DNA."

"*My* DNA? I don't get what you mean."

"Australian Aboriginal DNA is pretty pure. It appears to be of the most ancient bloodlines left on earth. Yours in particular is quite refined. It's been relatively easy to splice off the last generation. For forty thousand years, the Australian Aboriginal's DNA remained relatively untouched, and the DNA from the aliens that once roamed the earth is easy to find within it."

We entered a room that was bigger than an aircraft hangar—even bigger than the first cavernous space I had witnessed in that awful place—and had dim lighting.

It was filled with row upon row of steel cages.

Dark shadows moved around within those cages, and they let out soft rumbling growls and coarse, raspy breaths. I couldn't see much in the gloom, but the acrid stink of ammonia was so overwhelming my lungs screamed and my eyes watered.

Ice pumped through my veins and cramps gripped my legs as I struggled to follow Harding. Boots' heavy breathing thundered in my ears as he stalked close behind me to hand out the occasional not so gentle push in the back.

"Are you pumping acid or some shit into me?" I asked as the room continued to spin out of control.

Harding paused and turned around to gaze into my eyes. At first, I felt as if someone was massaging my brain, and then large, probing fingers poked at it. I gasped in shock and held my head between my hands as I tried to push that invisible finger away. I slumped against the wall and my eyes flicked to Harding again.

Her face had changed. Her full lips were now paper thin, and sported sharp little teeth along their top line. Thick, grey cords hung where her golden hair had shimmered but a moment ago.

I turned to try and get away, but I stumbled into Boots' iron chest. He pushed me back into the wall with a look of disgust. My eyes looked up to see Harding, but she once more appeared as her beautiful self, and without a single hair out of place.

"This... *this* is your prize fucking creature?" Boots scoffed. "Look at him. He's a piece of shit—there's not a fighting bone in his body."

"Well," Harding replied, "that is exactly what we are going to find out. Everybody has a motivator. What motivates Lance Corporal Pinfold? Besides, we need him scared. We need the adrenalin to bond with the DNA."

Boots pulled me up from the floor, and Harding straightened my coveralls. "I'm not pumping you *full* of acid, Pinny... just a small amount."

"So why is everything so fucking weird? Why won't the room stop spinning?"

"We are giving you higher and higher doses of pure alien blood. It will affect your physical characteristics and your senses. We can only give you the blood once your adrenaline levels are within an optimum range."

"My blood is mixed enough. I don't want any fucking more shit. I'm already a fucking freak!"

"Oh, my dear boy. Once we are finished with you... you will be an even more lethal soldier than our friend, Boots, here. Boots was our first real success story, mostly thanks to his relatively pure Germanic bloodline.

But, I can imagine, it's nowhere near as old or pure as yours," she told me as she gave Boots a warning glare.

"I don't want to be anything like that fuckwit. I want to go home." My words were thick on my tongue.

"Listen," Harding growled. "Just *fucking* listen!"

So, I listened, and the low growls I'd heard became a stream of voices. The soft roars, whispered shouts. I put my head between my knees and groaned. I couldn't understand the words, but it was definitely talking—talking to me.

"You *are* fucking home!" Harding hissed. Boots jerked me back to my feet and pushed me forward.

We went through another set of double steel doors and straight into a lift. The fluorescent lights forced me to clamp my eyes shut. Boots swiped his card and punched in a set of numbers—security was extra tight.

The elevator lurched along with my stomach; there was plenty to be said for being shut in a small space with Boots Bodean Perry, and none of it was nice.

Harding, on the other hand, ensured she was pressed up tight against me, and wriggling her delectable derriere against my body as she continued to speak.

Why do psychos always monologue?

"No, you're not on drugs. Although, thanks to LSD and cocaine, we were able to create some effective cover stories. Of course, not all experiments are successful.

Boots was one of our first volunteers, and he was a marvellous success story. Controllable yet ruthless—

Boots has abilities that far surpass your average human, and way beyond the average soldier. Unfortunately, there's always going to be collateral damage with such projects. Like your poor friend, Snowy, for example."

"Are you doing this for money?"

Harding hissed at my question under her breath.

"You humans think this is only ever about money. This is *bigger* than money. This is the future safety of your planet. Money and wealthy men are of no value to me—they don't fight wars. They just get richer, while the lower classes make dead heroes out of themselves.

It's the same all over. But, as I said, Pinny, it's not like anybody actually cares about this damn backwater anyway—or the people in it for that matter."

My body, unfortunately, had no compunctions about Harding being a psychopathic bitch, and quickly betrayed the profound disgust in which I viewed her.

Cocks have no conscience.

Fuck, I hoped the elevator wouldn't break down.

Chapter Eight

The doors finally pinged open. I rushed out and sucked in deep breaths of fresh air. *Fresh air*—no bleach or recycled ventilation. We were on the surface.

The sun was just starting to spill over the horizon.

The mosquitos swarmed, but I barely noticed their savage attack on my skin. Stretched out in front of me was an area the size of a couple of basketball courts with concrete walls some three stories high all around. In each corner sat guard towers equipped with machine guns of a sort I didn't recognise, manned by one of Harding's over-muscled goons.

The whole thing had been sunk into the ground, so that where the walls ended at the top, the jungle floor began. Razor wire rippled across the top of the walls in tight, one-foot square, criss-cross patterns. Over the top of that was spread a barrage of cam nets—this place would be invisible from the sky and inescapable from the ground.

"Here we are," Harding said.

"Where? What is this place," I asked, although I did not really want to know the answer.

"This, Pinny, is the training arena. It is where you decide if you want to live like a warrior or, well, *donate* your body to another worthy cause," she said with a warm smile that turned my insides into a sickening mush.

The elevator pinged and Macka and Chook tumbled out onto the dirt floor. They were followed by Mason and Johnny—the muscle-bound goons I'd met before.

"See, I told you Mr. Jacobs would get a fighting chance," Harding added.

I was so glad to see them both. I ignored Harding's teasing and ran to them straight away. Like me, both had a metal band around the back of their heads. The elevator pinged again, and I noticed Harding, Boots, and the other goons had disappeared.

"I just saw Wog-Boy... I just saw Wog-Boy have his dick ripped off by some alien thing," I sobbed, as the raw grief and terror of what I'd witnessed erupted at the sight of my mates.

"What do you mean, *some alien thing*?" Chook asked with disbelief in his voice.

"Aliens, man. This place is about *aliens*. They got cages and cages of the fuckers," I told him.

"Bullshit," swore Macka. His eyes were mere pinpricks—he was buzzed off his head. "They just slipped you some LSD or something, man. You're hallucinating.

They have some good shit." His grin was lopsided.

"I'm not making this shit up, Macka! I saw this alien bitch fuck Wog-Boy and then rip his dick off!"

"Are you okay, Pinny? You don't look so great, man." Chook tried to calm me down. He seemed torn between believing the unbelievable situation or Macka, the unbelievable *person*.

"No, I'm not fucking alright, man. I just told you what I saw," I snapped. For the first time, I noticed my skin had a strange, grey hue. Maybe it was just the way the sun filtered in through the canopy, perhaps not.

I'm an average sized bloke at five foot seven, and at eighty kilos, I always had more of a wiry build than bulk. But now, I was mesmerised by the muscles, which bunched in my forearms and rippled through the bulges of obvious biceps.

Shocked, I tried to catch Chook's attention. I realised I was now also looking *down* into Chook's eyes, and I could see the knobbly tip of his nose—he'd been taller than me only a few hours ago!

As my pulse surged, I could hear the soft surge of icy blood pumping through my arteries. I shook my head to try to shake the bullshit thoughts taking place in there.

"I dunno what kind of shit they're pumping into us—steroids maybe? Alien juice? That's what Psycho Bitch Harding said anyway. You saw what they did to Snowy.

Chook, these guys are a whole new level of crazy."

"Harding explained what happened," Chook

said.

"He just had an allergic reaction."

"Allergic reaction my ass!" I wondered why Chook was being so fucking stupid. "They're toying with us, man, playing games. We're going to fucking die unless we find a way out of here!"

Chook looked up at the vertiginous enclosure around us. "How the hell do you think we are going to do that Pinny?" he asked.

I slid closer to the wall and I saw massive claw marks slashed down the side of the rough concrete. I looked at Macka and pointed. "Still don't believe me?"

Some of the scratches almost reached the top. Burn marks were dotted randomly like bruises along the pockmarked, grey walls, and I noticed a large patch of the razor wire across the top sparkled like new. Maybe this is where that big beast we'd encountered—that *alien*—had escaped?

Holy Mary, Mother of Christ! I thought as I sunk into the muddy ground. What the hell had we done—or not done—to deserve this? My body trembled, and I couldn't control it.

"Look at this," Chook said as he poked his finger into one of the holes in a nearby column and teased out a bullet. My eyes grew large at the size of the round.

"Looks like something you'd hunt elephants with," I replied, and my guts started to churn again. We all turned our heads as the elevator pinged again. The door opened, and stayed open.

Then a familiar voice crackled over the Tannoy.

"Gentleman. Welcome to our training arena. In the lift, you will find a collection of weapons. You have one minute to arm yourselves as you see fit."

Arm ourselves? We all stared at each other blankly.

Macka smiled a goofy smile, started whooping, and ran around in circles. *What kind of bloody game is she playing at?*

"Is this some kind of joke?" asked Chook.

"I don't think so, mate. This is another one of her sick fucking games." I ignored the clenching in my gut and pulled Chook over to the lift. Shocked, I eyed the collection of rusty, ancient weapons—all designed for bloody hand-to-hand combat.

Fight off fucking aliens with an axe?

I grabbed a double-headed battle-axe from the top of the pile and dragged it out of the elevator and onto the ground, along with most of the contents of the elevator—just as its doors closed.

"What the hell is this shit?" I mumbled to myself as I sorted through the assortment of weapons: knives, swords, spears, and axes. No guns, no firepower—no fucking chance.

Chook flicked through the pile and collapsed onto his knees into the thick mud. "I don't know how to use any of this shit, I use a radio for

110

Christ's sakes. I mean... what is the point even?"

He was right, of course. I felt frustration, rage, and disgust building up in my stomach again; it smothered the fear that knotted there. This rage, raw and primal, was a new feeling—it was not one I was comfortable with. I tried to ignore Macka running around brandishing a sword like he was King fucking Arthur.

Why hadn't I been given what he'd had? He was at least going to die not giving a fuck. What the hell kind of game was Harding playing?

I looked down at the array of old weapons. Harding wants this to be bloody and horrible. Why? Why not just kill us cleanly?

Adrenaline. The bitch was trying to raise my adrenaline so she could infect me with more of that shit.

All of a sudden, Wog-Boy's situation didn't look quite so bad. You show me one guy who wouldn't prefer to be fucked to death by some stunning sex bomb, than mangled with a rusty old sword.

"Well, I'm not fighting you guys," I said with grim determination. I picked up a sheath of throwing knives and a smaller, double-sided axe. I found a short sword and thrust it into Chook's sweaty hands. "C'mon, mate.

She'll be right. If *we* don't have guns, *they* won't have guns." I looked into his eyes. It was bullshit, but it was *genuine* bullshit.

Chook nodded his head in dumb agreement

111

before asking, "But *who* Pinny? Who are we meant to be fighting?"

"I think the question here, Chook, is *what*? *What* are we fighting?" Macka chipped in.

Before I could answer, Harding's voice crackled loudly over the speaker.

"Gentleman, the rules are simple. You have five minutes to keep yourselves alive. Only five minutes. If you are still alive at the end of this test, then you will have fulfilled your purpose and will be free to ...leave.

Here is your fighting chance, Mr. Jacobs—you can thank Terence for this one."

I heard the soft ping of an elevator from the middle of the arena, and watched as four monstrous, human-like-creatures emerged. They squinted and rubbed their eyes as if dazed by the small shafts of sunlight.

"Holy shit, Pinny! What the hell are they?" Chook whispered.

I couldn't answer, but I'd swear one looked like the guys from the village the other day. My throat squeezed tight. Dressed in farmers' rags, the man-creatures each averaged a respectable six-foot, and their bodies were disjointed and misshapen, but unmistakably solid. One walked upright, two were grossly pulled askew and swaggered to one side—crippled almost. The fourth... the fourth just crawled along the floor like a lizard.

What the fuck were those things? Harding's

collateral damage?

The sound of my pulse flooded my ears, and my pounding heart beat away all tangible thought. I tried to shake my head clear, and that was when I heard Chook gulp. Loudly. My eyes zoomed in on the beads of sweat bursting on his skin, mesmerised as they popped to release the bitter stink of his fear.

Keep it together, man.

I rubbed my eyes as the world spun in and out of focus in slow motion. Curling forward, I tried to block out the crunch of our boots in the dirt. I dragged myself upright and tried to focus on the grotesque, man-like abominations in front of us. I froze. They had no weapons. I couldn't kill in cold blood.

I then remembered the craziness, and just how hard those in the village had been to kill— they were like the Berserkers. In the stories of the old Vikings, such things were killing machines with a bloodlust that blinded them to pain, reason, and mercy.

I shifted the axe to my other hand and picked up the shaft of a small spear. I tested its weight in my sweaty palm.

Like sleepy hounds vacating the comfortable confines of their kennel, the things appeared disorientated as they tried to hide their eyes from the sunlight. The movements of their cruelly deformed bodies were disjointed and shambolic.

One tilted his head to the sky, nostrils flaring at our scent. He turned his head in our direction, and all four went rabid at the sight of us. They released a blood-curdling yell and charged towards us, the muddy ground churning under their feet as they ran. I panicked as I threw the spear—my hand slipped and the spear flew well wide of the group.

Fuck!

I had no time to reach for another one. Macka let out a roar and raced off towards the man-creatures brandishing his broadsword. I tried to call him back, but knew there was no way we could pick them off one on one. He was off. Chook froze beside me, locked onto my side.

Macka came to a sudden halt, heaved the sword over his head, and threw it two-handed towards the things.

Sadly, throwing a sword is much more a practiced art then it appears, and Macka was just as high as a fuckin' kite and with no fucking idea whatsoever. We all watched as the sword spun tip over handle through the air...

The handle hit the lead creature and clattered harmlessly to the ground. Luckily, the three others, in their blind bloodlust, didn't see the falling blade and stumbled over it; they fell over in a crazy tangle of warped limbs.

Macka, seeing his plan had failed and he was now weaponless, came tearing back, his skin waxy and shining with sweat. He threw himself onto the pile of weapons with the twisted man-creatures hot on his heels.

I pulled Chook over, and we managed to form a little semicircle around the weapons just before the lead creature was upon us.

"Go for the guts, Chook!" I shouted as I sunk down low and swung my axe in a long arc into the thing's legs. My arms jarred as the axe blade carved through its shin and calf. The whole leg gave out as the fragile tibia and fibula snapped. Falling sideways, the man-creature clutched wildly at Chook and took him down with it.

Chook's sword ended up deep in the thing's guts.

Chook kept on, and wrenched the sword in a broad, circular motion until the man-creature's intestines spilled from its flanks. Resolutely, Macka brought his boot down onto the thing's head with relentless fury, cracking its skull. Despite this, the thing kept on moving.

I'd just pulled my axe free and stood up when the second man-creature fell on top of us. The entire left side of its body appeared flayed, as if the grotesquely bulging muscles had literally torn through the skin.

I used the axe handle like a staff to push the thing away until I had enough room to swing my weapon, and I barely noticed the cramping burn within my muscles.

The thing grabbed my axe handle with both hands, so I kicked out to pulp its testicles with a stellar blow, which I expected to leave it writhing on the ground. The force of the kick sent the man-creature staggering backward, but he paid no mind to the fact that his balls had just been smashed like fragile bird's eggs. He just came straight back into the melee.

Meanwhile, the metal bands on my, Chook's, and Macka's heads beeped out loud and in symphony.

Macka swung wildly with a large hunting knife he'd found, and managed to hold back Berserker Number Three.

Bones, I called him, 'cos his ribs pushed through his chest cavity so much you could see the bone. His leg muscles had, at some point, burst through his layers of scaly skin to leave strips of the underlying tissue exposed like fresh cuts of meat. The creature swatted away Macka's knife without any thought, and crash-tackled him to the ground.

Chook, having given up on retrieving his sword from the lead Berserker's stomach, grabbed a sledgehammer from the weapon pile and hammered at Bones' skull; the sick, squelching sound of pulped flesh and bone reverberated in my ears. Still, the creature scrambled to wrap his bloodied fingers around Macka's neck, even while twitching in its death throes.

The other creature tried to stop my wild axe swings, and at one point, I saw its hands were reduced to bloodied, broken, and severed fingers—and yet still he kept on coming. Up close, I saw the spider's web of black blood beneath the surface of his blistered skin.

Shivers shot down my spine. The thing seemed to see nothing; its face was a mask of pure hatred and fury.

Distorted with rage, its bloodied lips were torn back over the overly-large teeth he gnashed together in a God-awful chattering sound.

What the hell were these creatures?

In the corner of my eye, I saw Chook copy my axe move with his hammer. He smashed it hard into the side of the creature's knee bone. I heard the *crunch* and ripping of flesh, and the creature staggered sideways.

This caused me to over-reach with my axe and fall off balance, and I fell under the thing's outstretched arms and ended up behind it. There I was, sandwiched between two monsters and separated from my mates.

A needle-sharp pincer grip on my thigh made me cry out in pain as Number Four grabbed me. I turned with surreal speed and lashed out with my axe, which severed his arm below the elbow. I reeled a little bit from the shock of what I had just done, and the sight of blood spurting from the ragged stump. Then, I brought my arm back and ripped the axe into the thing's neck.

The axe came to a jerking stop halfway through. My arm wrenched at the socket as my hand slipped from the handle. I left it there, wedged in the poor bastard's neck.

In slow motion, I saw my blood-soaked hand in front of my own face, and it was a contorted, bony mess. I didn't recognize the large, gnarled fingers and gore-soaked claws that were so large, so strong, so not fucking mine.

The fight continued around me as I dropped to my knees and screamed in agony and terror, as my entire body seized in a cramp. The creature pulled the axe from its neck and grabbed me by the leg with his good hand; I felt nothing but ice flames rage through my body as he dragged me through the mud, and away from Chook and Macka.

I thought I heard my name called out, but I was oblivious to everything except the waves of seizures rippling through my body, my bones shattering, and ligaments snapping in a cascade of pure pain. I wanted to die, and to die quickly— I wanted that pain to end. I flopped around on the muddied floor for what seemed like an eternity, as the flesh was torn from my ankle, almost to the bone, where the creature still held me captive like a bear with a fish.

Then it stopped.

Oxygen hit my lungs like cocaine. It coursed through my body like electricity. I pushed myself up onto my clawed, deformed hands with a loud, guttural roar.

Chook, who had been running towards me, his

face a mess of blood and mud, came to a sudden halt. The look of sheer horror on his face was instantaneous. Macka, quick on his heels, jerked Chook backward and away from me.

Blood rushed through my body like an orgasm and I cried out in ecstasy.

I rose to my feet and kicked away the creature's hand like it was nothing. The thing turned to look at me, he hissed between broken teeth and sank back onto his haunches, as he prepared to spring.

Our bodies slammed together and I grappled him like he was a crocodile out on the mud flats. We were both slippery with mud, but I had claws— *fucking claws*—and they hooked deep and solid into his flesh to tear muscle away from bone.

The creature bucked and writhed underneath me as it rolled in the mud trying to crush me with his weight. I held on as he slammed my body into the earth, driving the air from my lungs in a massive *hmpfff*. With my diaphragm non-functioning, Miraculously, I managed to get my hand free. I tore at his face in a frenzy, relishing the feel of his skin peeling away beneath my claws.

Soon, his face, or what was left of it, hung in bloodied, stringy lengths from my fingers and I found I could breathe again. I found just enough room to jackhammer my knee into his stomach and lift the creature. I was then able to twist from under his body and throw myself on top. His face close to mine, the creature shrieked with fury and terror, and with the stinking breath of a decayed corpse.

I withdrew one arm once he was beneath me, and I hammered it into his face with all my weight behind it.

The feel of crushing, splintering of bone beneath my fist was almost erotic. Again, and again, I pummelled his skull until my freakish clawed hands ran thick with blood, bone, and brain.

It was only when the thing's grotesque body stopped twitching beneath my legs that I quit. I drew in a big breath and sighed in relief.

Then I remembered Chook and Macka. I watched them as they backed away towards the weapons pile, their faces contorted with fear. I tried to speak, but my words tripped and stumbled through a mouth with its too many teeth, and came out as a series of muffled grunts.

"Pinny, what the hell man?" Chook broke off at the pinging of the elevator. I lifted my head to view the elevator from which the abominations had come, only to be greeted with three more monstrosities. I sensed these were yet more developed and dangerous than the previous four—they were Berserkers in every sense of the word. Panicked, I ran back towards Chook and Macka.

My legs churned through the slick mud. I

stumbled, unused to the powerful momentum I had unleashed. But the new creatures were just as fast, if not faster, and one crash-tackled me into the slush.

I laughed, as it was no more painful than if the Berserker had hit me in the back with a pillow. I twisted underneath him, just as his fist connected with my jaw.

The force snapped my head back into the mud. Weird—it didn't hurt any more than getting walloped with a newspaper.

The world ran in slow motion as I bucked my hips enough to throw the thing off balance. Rolling over, I blew the mud out of my nose before catching his flailing fist mid-strike. I pulled him forward and slammed my open hand straight into his throat. I curled those claws into his flesh, and the cartilage cracked like an egg. His eyes bulged as he fought for air and tore frantically at my face and chest. My hand grabbed something soft and slippery... I yanked on it as hard as I could, and ripped his tongue out from the root. The creature's jaw dropped open in shock and he collapsed on top of me wracked by twitching spasms and gurgling of blood.

I pushed the creature off and saw Chook standing flat against one of the columns. He had Macka beside him.

His buzz had long gone, the cocaine burnt out through his system by shock, and his eyes pleaded with me for help as the massive creatures closed in on them. Poor Chook looked shattered as he dragged the short sword along the ground as the beastly creatures circled towards him.

I tried to call out and warn them, but what came out was a muffled roar. I felt something grab me. *What the hell!?* Scrambling to my feet, I kicked the dying Berserker's clutching hands off my legs and ran towards Chook and Macka.

I had to try and save them!

The surge of power I'd had dissipated at an alarming rate. My muscles quit responding, and I may as well have been running thigh-deep in setting concrete. Macka and Chook's eyes popped wide as I charged toward them. I'm not sure if I scared them any less than the Berserkers heading their way.

Stumbling and jelly-legged, I used the last of my strength to tackle one of the Berserkers to the floor. It easily regained control and threw me back into the mud.

Knuckles dug into my skull as the thing stretched me upwards. With one hand under my jaw, I knew it was going to try to snap my neck. I gasped and gurgled but all the fight had gone out of me, and I floated on the edge of consciousness.

Through the mud-splattered haze, I watched Chook and Macka exchange furtive whispers. At the last moment, as the one of the monsters committed his lunge at them, they split and darted away. They knew it was a fifty-fifty chance, and Chook lost. The creature shot his arms out and managed to clip him, which sent him spinning into the mud. The sword flew from his hand.

Chook moved fast. His hand clutched onto the spear I had mis-thrown earlier. He managed to plunge the thing directly into the Berserker's eye socket. The creature roared and flailed, which gave Chook just enough time to slip away and rearm himself with his sword.

Time had to be up, surely.

The Berserker pulled the spear from his eye with a terrific roar and gushes of viscous blood. With the spear in his hand, he stood there and looked around for Chook.

I couldn't see my mate either, until I caught Chook's shadow leaping over my body in my peripheral vision.

I was winded by the impact of his weight as he jumped onto our backs, and I felt the burn of the metal blade as it skewered our bodies together.

"Sorry!" he shouted as he drove that sword even deeper. "You don't want this kind of life, Pinny, I know you don't." He was actually weeping. On the precipice of death, I still couldn't decide; maybe it was better he had made the decision for me.

He'd lost his chance of escape. Chook landed back on the ground when the one-eyed Berserker grabbed his arm with both hands. He put one foot on Chook's squirming body and pulled. Blood fired back through my body with the painful sound of tearing muscles. Chook screamed out in pain as the monster ripped his arm from its socket. The beast held Chook's arm in one hand and picked him up by the throat...

Somewhere, a buzzer rang over the speaker and broke through Chook's screams.

Our five minutes were up.

Chook and Macka had survived. They would go free, yes?

"The trial is up. Please release your fellow combatant and return immediately to your entrance points,"

Harding instructed. Chook was still garbling in pain and flailing in the hands of the monster.

"Release the survivor *instantly* and return to your entrance point," Harding commanded the Berserker holding Chook. It shot a look of contempt over its shoulder at us and snarled before zeroing back in on Chook to crush his windpipe with large, meaty fingers.

Chook jerked and writhed before slumping in the thing's hand. Tears of frustration burnt my eyes. What the fuck?

It wasn't fair. We had survived. We had played her fucking game.

A booming shot rang out across the arena. A grappling hook punched through the back of the rogue Berserker, its claws exploding through his chest. A look of shock flashed across the thing's face and it dropped Chook as a whirring noise sounded, and it was dragged back across the arena floor towards the far guard tower like a fish on a silver line.

Macka ran over to Chook's ruined body, his body buckling with grief and anger. I tried to move, but my body didn't respond. *Oh, my God, am I paralysed?* My brain screamed at my body to react... but there was nothing.

The rogue Berserker was now pinned up against the guard tower in the opposite corner. I heard the elevator ping. Harding and Boots stepped into the arena with a couple of goons I recognized from before—Johnny and Mason—hot on their heels.

Macka unleashed a hellish war cry and ran over to them. Harding didn't even blink as she ducked under the axe he swung at her. Mason and Johnny stepped forward and deftly caught Macka under an arm each, as if they had practiced the manoeuvre a thousand times, and carried him away to the elevator.

Macka screamed help, but I could do nothing; it was as if my body was sunk in concrete—I couldn't do a fucking thing but watch them throw Macka into the elevator before the doors closed behind them.

I lay sobbing into the mud. I was a worthless piece of shit, an abomination, a monster that couldn't even save my mates.

Then Boots' shadow fell over me. I felt the bite of a needle in my arm.

Chapter Nine

I woke to an icy blast of high-pressure water blasting on my face and needling my body. I groaned with the agony of my bruised flesh and the feeling that my skull was being crushed between two rocks. With limbs of rubber, I floundered pathetically against the surge of water.

I lay there, naked and helpless as a new-born baby, unable to comprehend what had happened to me. I remembered, though, I'd had a fucking spear through my chest! My hands clutched at my chest, searching for the raw, gaping wound, but there was nothing more than an angry red scar and a dull, bruising throb.

I was relieved to find myself back in my own skin at least, and alive. My hands were no longer deformed and clawed, or my muscles—they were still a lot larger than they had ever been— long and sinewy. Maybe it had all been a damn good hallucination from the drugs I was sure they were pumping into us— *alien blood, DNA, crazy shit!*

Chook!

The water stopped and a pathetic, wailing noise filled the void. I realised it was me.

"Get dressed, Lance Corporal Pinfold. There's a bed there. Catch some shut-eye. We'll be back for you soon enough," barked a faceless voice. I heard the hosepipe hit the floor and whoever owned the voice left the room.

I heard a key turn the lock, and the tumblers fall into place.

I rolled onto my hands and knees, and rested there until the room stopped spinning. I panted with the effort.

The arena seemed like a lifetime ago, but the mud and blood crusted in my fingernails said different. I vomited, as the wet *schlucking* sound of pulped Berserker brain replayed in my mind.

Chook...

Climbing to my feet, I shut the thought away. Did it even happen, or was it part of one very fucked up, drug-induced nightmare?

The room was another small cubicle. It was clinical, cold, concrete, and much like every other room I'd seen in the place. I collapsed onto the bed, pulled the thin blanket over my wet, naked body, and closed my eyes. I tried to push away all the crap that threatened to overwhelm me.

I failed.

I kept looking at my hands, which trembled as they had since my first tour. But there was no sign of those beastly claws I'd seen in the arena. Like the rest of the larger and stronger me, my hands were familiar, but not quite mine.

I'd been stoned before; smoked a little bit of grass. I always stayed away from the hard drugs—I saw what they did to people, black and white, and I never wanted to lose myself like that. I hadn't felt *stoned* in the arena, though, I had been terrified as shit and running on adrenaline. Then there had been the rage, a boiling, bubbling rage as I beat that *thing's* head to a pulp. I don't ever remember feeling rage like that before. Not even when Jenny...

Jenny, was she safe? Was Harding telling the truth, or did I just want it to be the truth?

Exhaustion tugged at every muscle in my body, but still, the stream of thoughts chugged on. Apparently, what I wanted, and when I was going to get out of this situation were two entirely different things. Although, glancing at my naked body under the sheets, I couldn't hate this fit, muscular new body. But how long would it be before I imploded like Snowy or turned into an ass-fuck like Boots?

One thing I'd learned in the arena was there is no point being bigger and stronger than your opponents unless you could save your mates. So far, on that score, I'd failed dismally.

The whole war being a set-up hadn't seemed quite as far-fetched as the whole alien thing, but then again, I had actually *seen* them. Those things in the cages had fucking spoken to me! I'd even seen poor bloody Wog-Boy get fucked to death by one of them, what more proof did I need?

Okay, so aliens are real. But was Harding right? Was there some invading alien army on the horizon we were ill-equipped for? Shit, we could barely fight the enemy we were *supposed* to be fighting in this fucking hell-hole—we were too busy fighting ourselves. It looked to me like we were destined to be wiped out as a species.

Besides, if it meant becoming one of them to beat them, I didn't know if I wanted to survive.

I dozed on and off for God knows how long until they came and got me. I noticed with some satisfaction how the goons kept a respectful distance as they escorted me through the rabbit warren of corridors until I arrived at Harding's office door. A quick knock, they pushed me through the door and shut it behind me.

Harding was at her desk, looking sexy as hell, and clapping her hands together in slow applause. "Well done, Pinny, you certainly are impressive."

"I don't know what you mean, Harding. Where's Chook and Macka? Where are my mates?"

Harding frowned. "What, you don't remember?"

"I don't know what I remember. You're pumping all these fucking drugs into us."

"I didn't put any drugs in you, Pinny," she said.

"Chook didn't survive the arena. Well, *technically* he did, but accidents happen, right? Let's just call him collateral damage."

"Accident? Collateral fucking damage?" Memories of my mate's death flooded my mind. "One of your fucking monsters ripped his fucking

129

arm off and crushed his throat! You call that a fucking *accident*?!"

"It's one of the problems we have with our current formula. The Berserkers aren't as obedient as we would like, and sometimes they go rogue. They simply lack self-control and discipline. We're expecting this is something we can do better with you. Progress is already looking positive."

"Fuck your progress. I don't want any part of this."

"Oh, but you already are, Pinny. Your transformation is already fifty percent complete. Soon you'll be practically invincible, a marvellous military asset. A god amongst men."

"You're crazy, absolutely fucking *cuckoo*, woman.

What the hell have you done with Macka? Are you turning him into a God as well?"

Harding smiled—that icy bitch smile that turned my legs to water, despite my rage.

"You'll see Macka soon. His DNA isn't as pure as yours. So, he'll be undertaking a different type of transformation. I don't think he'll be too happy to see you, though, not after you just laid there and watched my men take him away."

"I didn't just fucking lay there! I was paralysed and I had a fucking sword through me! What the hell happened out there? What the hell is happening *here*?"

Harding sighed dramatically, "Aliens, Pinny.

Aliens are what's happening here. Earth is not on the outskirts of the civilised universe anymore. The human species are such weak, fragile creatures—you'll be destroyed before you can even blink. We need to be ready, and if it costs a few lives, then so be it."

"*A few lives*? They're my mates." Anger burned in my belly.

"Friends, family, lovers... they will destroy them all, Pinny. I'm trying hard with what little we have to save this planet. It's not pretty, it's not sensitive, but it is what needs to be done."

"Are you fucking insane?! I don't know what the hell happened out there, but if you've turned me into one of those *things*, just kill me now! I want nothing to do with that... those *abominations*."

Harding's head snapped back as if I'd slapped her, and her eyes blazed ice. She slid off the table, walked over and opened the door. Outside, waiting, was Boots' asshole of a face.

"I've risked so much. I've made you a God amongst your people, and you insult my sanity," she said. "Come with me, Pinny, so you can see what insanity really is."

Chapter Ten

With Harding leading the way and Boots breathing down my neck, we moved once W more through the building, back to near the elevator, back to that dark area filled with cages. Now, though, it was full of light and action.

I recognised the *Bututus*—more commonly known as Bigfoot—squatting in their sizeable communal cell.

The ape-like creatures stood upright like humans and were coated in thick, black hair. The skin on their noses, cheeks, and the female's bare breasts appeared green.

Their eyes were pensive and resigned.

My heart broke for them. I'd heard reports from the Americans, and some New Zealand forces, of Bututus being spotted in the more mountainous areas of Vietnam. I'd thought at the time it has been just a hoax.

"They *are* real," I gasped.

"Those... *apes*? Yes." Harding said. "The original research facility was set up to study the primitive creatures back in the 1950s. Pacifists the lot of them—totally useless as soldiers, and nothing more than pets now. Though, I must admit they've contributed quite significantly to our genetic programming of what we call our Beast Boy soldiers." She indicated various cages within the structure.

Unlike what I'd faced outside, those things less resembled men and more monster. They had long, razor-sharp claws and vicious-looking mouths that had far too many teeth packed inside.

"You used freshwater crocs as well?" I asked. The odd few creatures were covered in thick hair like the Bututu's, while several others had patches of reptilian skin. I remembered the guard who'd brought us in, the thick hair covering his body, and the scales on Boots' neck.

"The more ancient and pure the blood line, the better.

We even added a few lizards to the mix. It's a species which is able to regrow limbs—it's a true find and a salute to your alien ancestry."

"What do you mean: *alien ancestry*?"

Shock flashed across Harding's face. "Oh, I keep forgetting your species are exceedingly ignorant of your development. The human race, *species* per say, was created by the Enki, who came from a planet not too dissimilar to Earth. Their planet was on the verge of destruction, so the Enki merged their DNA with the pre-existing Neanderthal species here. The subsequent jump in evolution made it possible for the Enki to survive on earth, and eventually flourish.

"Obviously, though, their higher intelligence became diluted and compromised over the generations.

133

Interestingly, though, Enki are 98.4% genetically compatible to the Ectronites that were found at the crash site. Hence, you are so compatible with Ectronite DNA.

It appears the Australian Aboriginal population did not lose the purer strains of Enki intelligence." Harding sounded quite enthusiastic about the whole thing, her mood having shifted in a heartbeat—that's women for you.

I snapped back to reality. The caged beasts snarled when they saw us enter, eyes growing wide, claws flexing.

"We've used the best, most humanoid of these things to train in our Super Soldier program, one of our American scientists christened them *Berserkers*. Like yours, their DNA has been spliced and melded. But unlike you, it's a messy, complicated procedure, and they have been placed within hosts until birthing. Same with these over here."

Dr. Harding walked to another area. I stood there in awe, looking at the beasts within the cages, several of which had the same alluring look as Betty. I saw their form shift and flicker into that of the most beautiful women. Others appeared to be mutations somewhere between human and alien—they were disjointed, misshapen creatures, their hue a mixed palette of blues and greys. Harding walked up close to one of the cages.

"These darlings are our hybrids. They are a

different class of Berserkers that are more... controllable. This is the programme Corporal Azzopardi has donated himself to. They grow to adulthood within months—some of them—and only the strongest and fiercest survive whelping, let alone reach adulthood. Look." The large, grey beast was dropped into a segregated cage by means of a mechanical cuff around its thick neck. "There's Betty. If we come back in thirty minutes or so, she should be ready to whelp."

My stomach knotted as my tentative grip on reality slipped away. My legs quaked beneath me and I clung to a wall to steady myself.

Harding must have misread me—or chose to.

"Yes, their gestation period *is* amazing. The information we gain about these creatures every day is simply fascinating." She smiled warmly at me, but I no longer saw seduction in her face.

"Yeah, fascinating," I mumbled. I felt decidedly numb as I followed on behind her shapely ass, and was all too aware of the tension emanating from Boots behind me.

"Quite. In here we have Charlie. He's the third of the original six we found alive. Charlie is an Ectronite, the genetic cousin of your ancestor, the Enki. He's one of the two remaining males we found on the crash site. We named the other alien Delta. We tried breeding Betty with Delta, and since she treats all her men the same, Charlie is all that we have left. Isn't he *magnificent*? Oh, I forgot, you actually got to meet Charlie earlier, out in the jungle. The naughty boy tried to escape." She let out a light laugh and a mischievous glint flittered in her hypnotic eyes.

My knees lost all their strength as I gazed at the double-barred steel cage in the middle of the room—and the beast within. I recognised the creature we'd encountered out there in the jungle, but something didn't quite fit. This creature was at least two and a half meters tall and was clearly an entirely different species to Betty.

Charlie was at least a whole metre taller, and I'd say had two-hundred kilograms on the female who'd so effortlessly destroyed Wog-Boy. Charlie looked like some kind of weird dinosaur with human-esque arms and hands, thick claws, and was standing on his hind legs. It even had opposable thumbs. But, despite his bulk, Charlie seemed far more lithe and slender than any of the dinosaurs in the books I'd read growing up— and looked way deadlier than even the most fearsome T-Rex.

"He's a different species to Betty, isn't he?" I asked with genuine curiosity.

"Yes. Betty is from Carfete, Charlie here is from a smaller planet—Ectron."

"How do you know that? And how did they end up at the same crash site?"

"We have our ways." Harding replied. "It was an Ectronite ship. Why the Carfetes were on it is still unclear. It's Charlie's blood you've been receiving, by the way."

I swallowed down the lump in my throat. Of course, he's the cousin to my ancestral DNA.

"So, how did they escape from here?"

"*They*? Only Charlie escaped."

All the while, Harding watched my reactions. She scanned her little metal bar over the thing in the back of my neck, and jotted down copious notes.

The creature paced his cage. He growled and bared his teeth with menace at Dr. Harding, his nostrils flaring at her in disgust. Charlie's face seemed quite human; it was flat rather than having an elongated snout like some lizard's. Charlie's behaviour also struck me as rather humanoid and there was an intelligence that shimmered in his eyes.

He sniffed the air and turned to look at me. His eyes, those pale blue, icy eyes so full of intention, burnt into me as if he was searching for something. Pins and needles prickled over my brain, causing me to squint in pain. I gasped as my knees finally turned to jelly beneath me. Harding stepped in between us and faced Charlie down, and the vibrations of his growl echoed in my mind rather than my actually *hearing* it. I was both terrified and mesmerised.

"Oh, that's interesting," Harding commented as she took yet more notes.

"He's not a fan of yours, is he, Dr. Harding?" I offered. The joke sat raw on my dry throat as I struggled to find my feet again.

Charlie's agitation had intensified in the presence of the doctor and her thick-set minder, and I felt the tension in the room brewing like an electrical storm.

"No, he's not a fan, Pinny," said Dr. Harding as she scribbled in her notebook. She turned to gaze at Charlie like a lover, her handsome face breaking into a beautiful smile. "The alien is torn between wanting to fuck me and wanting to rip my head off. He blames me for Delta's death and has not been particularly cooperative in his assistance with the program." The doctor stared at the alien through the bars of the cage the same way women watch men at the gym; her eyes were predatory and thick with lust.

"I can understand him wanting to rip your head off, but wanting to—"

Harding cocked her head to one side and stepped up close against me. Her wet, lush lips were mere centimetres from my own.

"Why do you find it so hard to believe that something would want to fuck me? Even you reek of sex pheromones when you look at me. I feel you undressing me with your eyes. I can see you fucking me in your mind."

"How can you smell my pheromones?" I was painfully aware of the effect Harding was having on my body.

"Never mind, Pinny." She sighed and ran a cool finger down my cheek and across my lips.

There came an ear-splitting growl. Charlie slammed hard into the bars of his cage. I'd been so memorised by Harding, I'd almost forgotten about the beast next to us, and I jumped.

Harding chuckled. "Don't get so jealous, Charlie," she mocked him with her sultry voice. She pulled on my hand in excitement. "Come look over here, let me show you our Super Soldier program. This is where Mackenzie has been assigned." She pointed across the expansive room to the broad side of the wall.

There were six standard barrack rooms, all with one-way mirrors. Each room was separated by partition walls, and much like the room I'd been in earlier, each one was pristine white and contained with a single bed.

At the end of the six rooms sat a large gaming room—it was a typical setup, but the occupants and the activities inside were anything but.

"This is our Super Soldier project," Harding continued. "Volunteers are injected with a mix of alien and Bututu blood, along with lashings of ecstasy and cocaine. Large volumes of testosterone and steroids are also part of the mix. It's a volatile and unpredictable combination, which creates equally volatile and unpredictable soldiers. They need to be given regular doses, or they would simply not survive each other; they are perfect for suicide missions or cannon fodder, but not so great for public relations."

There were ten men in the room. Each one was built like he'd spent a lifetime pumping iron and steroids. A few had the same pale grey skin as Charlie, while the rest looked far too human. Bile burnt the back of my throat as I recognised Macka sprawled face down on his belly across the pool table. One of the beefy guys was viciously buggering him, while the others paced around the table, all impatiently awaiting their turn.

Mercifully, Macka didn't look to be in pain, despite the bright splashes of blood that covered his naked buttocks and his assailant's lower belly. As I watched, my comrade's muscles twitched and expanded beneath his taut skin as he transformed into something altogether inhuman and *different*.

"Naturally one of the side effects of these chemical combinations is a heightened sex drive. Then, sometimes the Alien blood just doesn't take well, and we end up with deformed, terminal creatures,"

Harding explained, "like your friend Private Snow—though he was also severely short of the adrenaline needed to bond the DNA. Asian blood, despite its age, is no good—they have traces of another species. But blood like yours..."

I pretended not to hear, as I was trying not to think about the creatures I'd fought earlier, or the Berserker that hadn't even flinched when it ripped off Chook's arm before crushing the life out of him.

I'd never felt more useless in my life as I stood there watching poor Macka. His face slipped through expressions of terror, delight, insanity, and pain, and there was nothing I could do to help the poor bastard; as I watched him become less Macka and more beast, the less I wanted to.

I loathed myself at that moment, but I've never lied about being an abject coward; I just wanted to get the fuck out of there.

Against all instinct, I just couldn't tear my eyes away from Macka. There was just something endlessly fascinating in the way his skin colour turned into a sickly, greyish hue, and how his eyes narrowed into thin slits.

"Is this what happened to me?" I asked Harding.

"Oh, yeah," she drawled, "but you're undergoing a more specialised transition. Most unprecedented." As the man fucking Macka's ass finished up, Macka spun around and gave him a full-force, cracking punch to the jaw. The guy didn't even flinch. He just laughed out loud. The laugh sounded horribly familiar.

"These are the bastards you sent after Charlie. Are they the fuckers that killed Doc... and Taz?"

"Yes, they got distracted, I'm afraid," Harding said.

"Remember what I said about lack of self-control? They *are* improving, but they do believe all is fair in, what do you say... *love* and war."

141

Harding smiled as the Berserker returned my comrade's punch with one of his own. It sent Macka flying ass over tit across the pool table with his shattered jaw hanging slack.

Two of the Berserkers held down Macka's arms while a third sprung up onto the table and sat astride his bloodied, naked hips. Grinding himself hard against Macka, he leant forward and grabbed a couple of the pool balls off the green baize. As he did so, Macka took advantage of the momentary lapse, twisted his head around, and ripped its ear off with his teeth.

The tearing of flesh made the Berserker rear back with a surprised expression on his twisted face; Macka lifted his head off the pool table and smashed it into his nose.

The Berserker lost his balance and was pulled away from Macka by another who jumped on to my friend's broken body. Macka spat the severed ear at him in defiance. The Berserker grabbed it, and while grinding away on top of Macka, he ate it.

"Your DNA is being fused with Charlie's DNA—
using adrenaline as a type of glue. Whereas Macka here... he's just been infused with a little bit of everything. It doesn't always work, but mostly it does. Well, enough anyway."

My stomach rebelled completely at this point. I let fly with a projectile of bile. I collapsed to my knees, as each uncontrollable retch felt like a donkey kick to my solar plexus. Harding just tutted her disapproval and gestured for somebody to please come and clean my mess up.

I glanced up just in time to catch Macka thrusting his hips upwards to meet the man's bare ass to sodomise him.

"What the hell is going on here?" I wiped my face on my sleeve. "This is just fucking sick. Holy shit, Macka. Why aren't I in there with him? Why are you playing these games with me?"

"Because you are special, Pinny," Harding purred.

"Your body has reacted to the alien blood in a way we never imagined possible. The more ancient the blood, the better, we knew that. But, *wow*. Of course, there are a few more kinks to work out…"

I spun on my heel and pushed Harding up against the glass. I could taste salty tears on my tongue. "I don't want to be fucking *special*. I don't want to be a part of this… this… *freakshow*."

Boots grabbed my shoulder and yanked me off Harding. He raised his fist to pound my skull in.

"Stop!" Harding commanded. "He cannot handle another transition just yet, nor losing more blood."

Boots let me go with great reluctance.

"Oh gosh! Betty!" Harding exclaimed. "She must be ready to whelp by now. You *must* come and watch—it's really quite an amazing process." She smiled and dazzled me with her beauty.

"You're a fucking psychopath." I stopped Dr. Harding dead in her sick enthusiasm.

"Sorry, what did you say?" Dr. Harding asked. She lifted a quizzical eyebrow, which reminded me of just how dangerous she could be. I was done, though. I just couldn't process any more; I wasn't getting out of this, not alive, not human.

"I don't want to see anything else in your disgusting sideshow, or listen to any more of your bullshit fantasies." I squared up to the woman. "What you are doing here is a vile abomination. And why are you forcing me to watch my mates suffer?" In desperation, I grabbed Boots' rifle and jammed the cold barrel up under my chin. Boots didn't even resist; he just smiled.

"Just fucking kill me already." Sobbing, I reached for the trigger; I didn't want to be one of Harding's abominations.

The doctor placed her hand gently over mine. Her eyes filled with sympathy, she pushed the gun away from my jaw,

"I can't do that. And I know you don't have the balls to do it either." She smiled.

A part of me died inside as I realised she was right; I was so weak it was pathetic.

I felt Boots' vice-like grip on my shoulder and pain shot all the way down my spine. I smelt his breath—worse than any high school urinal—as he whispered in my ear,

"You will do whatever Dr. Harding wants,

nigger, or I promise I'll make what happened to Macka seem like a romantic dinner for two. And, I will *personally* ensure that Jenny and your son get a front row seat."

"Now, now, don't go making promises you can't keep," Dr. Harding chided the bastard.

Chapter Eleven

My legs felt like concrete pillars as we retraced our steps back to where Betty was about to give birth to little Wog-Boys. I remember Wog-Boy telling me about his son, Vince, back home in Melbourne. That kid was everything a father could ask for, and Wog-Boy adored him. Oddly enough, though, I sensed he wouldn't be quite so affectionate towards his offspring with that alien bitch.

We rounded the corner, and we faced the cage again. This time, sprawled out on the floor, was a semi-conscious Wog-Boy. I could see clearly the pain and confusion on my comrade's face. His jaw hung slack, swollen with black-purple bruising where it had dislocated. There was a large, bloodied bandage around his groin; it looked like a cheap pair of Y-Front jocks you pick up from Bones Department stores for 50c. It was bright red with splashes of blood blooming from the inside. I wanted nothing more but to cradle my friend's head and tell him everything was gonna be alright, and that I'd get him the hell out of there... but of course, that was impossible.

Wog-boy's head lolled to one side to face me, and I saw the recognition in his eyes—the acknowledgment of my abandonment. The pain and anguish I felt was as if my heart was being wrenched out through my mouth.

Wog-Boy began to convulse. His body spasmed in jerky, violent flexes.

"Betty has already placed the eggs. Sorry you missed that, Pinny," Dr. Harding said with nonchalance as she pointed to Wog-Boy's fractured jaw. She even managed to sound disappointed for me. I couldn't answer her; I was entirely out of words.

As I watched, Wog-Boy's stomach ruptured with a gushing explosion of blood, slop, and guts. He screamed out in ear-splitting agony, and I tried my damnedest not to look. But Boots stood at my shoulder with his body pressed close onto mine. With a steady, meaty hand on the back of my head, he forced it forward. I closed my eyes to shut out the sight, but the pinch of a sharp blade in the back of my neck and a whispered promise of slicing my eyelids off had me opening them in an instant.

It never ceases to amaze me what a man will do to prolong his life for as long as possible, even on the verge of such a tortuous death.

And so, I watched.

I watched as six little heads and a dozen tiny, sharp-clawed hands ate and clawed their way out of my friend's twitching body. I tried to vomit, but there was nothing left; all I wanted to do was fall to my knees and fade away, but the sharp blade digging into my side was just enough pain to keep my attention. I heard the beeps of my headgear and the bite of Boots' needle into my neck.

All the fight left me. Tears and runny snot flowed freely down my face as I wept for my friend.

Now, his jaw hung limp and his voice fell silent.

Wog-Boy had finally found his freedom.

Harding was about to speak when the sharp blast of air raid sirens pierced the facility. Boots put his knife away and re-armed himself with his rifle. He flicked off the safety and clenched the weapon tight. Bright, garish lights began blinking from every corner of the room, and for the first time since making her cold-hearted acquaintance, I saw Dr. Harding look frightened.

"No, no, no. Not now!" She stepped over to a large glass-covered panel that read EMERGENCY. Silently following her lead, Boots rammed the butt of his rifle into the glass to shatter it. Harding leaned over him and punched a code into the keyboard.

One red light went up. Then two.

Realizing I had a little less of their attention, I stepped back and away as the cacophony in the room became deafening as the alien beasts around us shrieked and roared in accompaniment to the sirens.

Harding still hadn't taken her eyes off the control panel, so I stepped back still further until I was in line with the rows of cages and out of her – and Boots' – line of sight. I saw a third red light blink on the panel, and suddenly all the beasts around me convulsed and collapsed lifeless to the floor of their cages. All except for the little Wog-Boys. They just kept on eating my friend's corpse, ripping at his flesh with needle-sharp teeth in their frenzy—and if one dared venture too close to another, they tore into each other like rabid animals.

"This is a code ONE-ONE-ALPHA. Please proceed to your nearest extraction point," a disembodied voice blasted through the Tannoy system on a continual loop.

Seizing my opportunity, I hauled ass as far away from Harding and her goon as possible. Of course, I had no idea what was going on, or what I was going to do, but for the first time in my life, it sure as hell felt better than doing nothing. Behind me, Boots yelled out, and a couple of rounds ricocheted off the cages around me.

I threw myself to the ground and wriggled my way along until I noticed I was now opposite the Berserker dorm—they were pounding hard on the door to get out. I espied a once familiar face staring out at me; Macka, barely recognizable, but it was still Macka. My stomach lurched as he recognised me. Instead of seeing relief, friendship, and the scream for help in his eyes, I saw a voracious predator hungry with bloodlust and revenge. My blood curdled.

Hating myself, I stood up and bolted towards

the nearest door.

Unfortunately, Boots was suddenly standing in front of it with his rifle locked and pointed at me.

"There you are, you cheeky shit. We ain't finished with you yet," he drawled with a broad grin on his face. Harding rushed up behind him, looking flushed, out of breath and still sexy as hell. She carried a heavy metal crate and a briefcase.

She glared at me sharply. "Don't worry about him, Boots, we have pretty much all we need from him; we know what to look for now. Here." She hefted the metal crate into his arms. Boots slung his rifle and shunted it over his shoulder, grunting at the weight of the crate.

"What are we going to do with him? We didn't prime him with a kill switch?" the goon grunted.

"Well, the Berserkers will be out soon," Harding replied as she punched codes into a hidden panel by the door. "I'm sure they'll sort him out, and if they don't, the facility will be wiped from the face of the earth in ten minutes. The fail-safe has been activated and everything will be incinerated. Russia will not extract any intelligence from this site. No, make that eight minutes now." She frowned as she glanced at her watch.

"Best of luck, Pinny." Harding smiled. "It's a shame we reached such an anti-climax, I had some fun things planned for us." And then she disappeared through the door.

Boots smiled at me. It was a cold, lifeless smile.

"Y'all have fun now, soldier." He laughed as the door shut behind him with a hiss.

Chapter Twelve

I searched frantically around. There had to be another way out. I heard a massive *crack* as the Berserkers I burst their way through the door. I glanced over and saw Macka—he was waiting patiently at the back of the room as the others smashed themselves to a pulp trying to push through the door. Macka just locked eyes with me and smiled. He blew me a kiss. I shuddered—I sure as hell didn't want to be around when he got out.

I kept moving, trying to put as much space between the Berserkers and myself.

I scanned the hall around me. Despite getting away from Harding and her bully-boy, my chances of survival had not improved by much. In fact, they may have even lowered, but at least I could take some action—anything would be better than falling into the hands of Macka and his new mates.

But there were no places to hide, and I didn't think with just seven minutes to go I had the choice to do so.

But, seven minutes and getting blown to shit had to be better than two minutes being buggered and shredded to shit by a my old friend and a bunch of Berserkers!

Around me, there were nothing but rows of

cages housing lifeless alien/human creatures; their putrid corpses reeked only marginally more now than they had in life. Still, it was a place to hide.

Maybe it was because of the evacuation, or the fact the creatures were dead now, but all of the cages had switched to manual. Yanking one open, I jumped inside and pulled the door shut firmly behind me. I approached the dead creature with caution; there was definitely no sign of life, and there was a large froth of bluish liquid oozing out from a white rip of flesh on its neck. I figured Harding and her cohorts had attached a small explosive to the thing's collar, which she'd detonated when the evacuation sounded.

My hands flew to my head as I remembered the band on my head. Holy shit, thank God, whatever the thing did, it wasn't a kill switch!

I didn't have time to investigate the creature's corpse further as the sound of the Berserkers' shrieking howls and whoops of maniacal excitement loomed closer by the second. All but puking at the rank odour of the dead alien, I pulled the corpse on top of me; its skin felt disgustingly similar to that of the wild boar I used to hunt. Although the putrescent stench of the creature was overwhelming, I pulled it down around me just as the Berserkers ran by.

There was nothing more I could do but try and survive. At least until Harding's bomb tore me to pieces.

What—or who—would make Harding and Boots turn tail and run? The Russians? Surely the Super Soldiers Harding had created would have given them the upper hand? Surely the Ruskies didn't have aliens...

I didn't want to be alive to find out. If something runs, it's because there's something bigger and uglier after it. I didn't want to experience bigger and uglier—I'd had enough.

The Berserkers charged past me. I had no idea of their intentions, or indeed if they had any understanding in their addled brains as to what was happening. I just prayed to God the explosion would find me before those bastards did. From the safety of the dead alien's arms, I watched as they ran around in a panicked frenzy. Once the half-human things realised the door was locked, they hit a crescendo of panic and took their fury out on each other, slashing, punching, and biting.

I heard a loud, metallic clang above the cacophony of the sirens, and caught sight of a bloodied, torn uniform two cages across. It was Macka, and he appeared still human enough to think straight. He inspected each pen as if he'd second-guessed my course of action. The others followed his lead, as Macka planned to find me and exact his revenge upon the comrade who'd left him to die.

There came a gut-churning roar, and in an instant, the game changed.

Charlie was here.

It was impossible—wasn't it? Why hadn't Charlie been killed along with the aliens? I couldn't bear to watch, yet I couldn't turn my eyes away as he flung the Berserker who'd entered his cage against the bars; the Berserker hit them so hard its bones shattered against the metal.

Leaping from his cage, Charlie launched himself at the Berserkers, and blood and torn flesh flew about the room. The Berserkers counter-attacked Charlie like savages, their bare hands grabbing at him and tearing at his body.

I pulled the dead alien around me like a grim comforter, and prayed for the explosion to wipe me and this hell into oblivion. You don't survive this; nobody wants to survive this.

I gripped the beast's body and pulled it tight around my ears to block out the grunts and screams of agony as the Berserkers attacked in their blind rage. Wailing shrieks were broken only by the sound of rending flesh, snapping bones, and the dull thud of lifeless bodies.

Limbs missing, bellies eviscerated and spewing blood, the Berserkers still kept up their relentless attack on Charlie.

Only when there was no life left in them at all did they stop; they just kept on with their mindless assault, no matter how futile it was against Charlie's superior size and strength. Charlie was invincible; he had all the weapons at his disposal—those claws and teeth, and that seemingly impenetrable skin. He just hacked through the writhing mound of Berserker flesh like they were paper dolls.

I registered the sound of heavy footsteps in my cell. I heard the cackle of laughter, and instantly recognized it as Macka's—only this wasn't Macka anymore.

The brute that had once been my brother-in-arms pulled away my protection. He yanked the dead weight of the alien corpse off me in a display of unnatural strength. He leaned in to study me, and up close, I saw his pupils were mere pinpricks—he looked stoned.

Terrified, I crawled up against the side of the cage and wished for a quick death that refused to come.

Instead, Macka paced the end of the pen and looked at me. his fists clenched and unclenched, and he appeared to be arguing with himself.

"Macka, mate... please don't do this," I begged. Where was the goddamn explosion? I didn't want to die like this...

Macka's body, now wrapped in thick, bulky muscle, rippled. Maybe the transformation hadn't been completed. Perhaps the Macka I knew was still in there?

"Macka, we've got to get out of here! This place is going to explode!" I shouted.

He snarled and snapped his teeth like an animal, then charged towards me and picked me up by the throat. His fingers, now immensely thick and powerful, dug deep into my windpipe as he smashed me against the metal bars like I weighed nothing at all.

"You left me! You let me become one of *them*, you bastard!" Macka struggled to form the words. I couldn't breathe. Lights flashed behind my eyes. I saw a sea of red just as Macka dropped me to the floor.

"Look what the fuckers did to me, you bastard!" He growled as he ran thick, meaty fingers over his face.

I nodded my head and desperately sucked in air through my crushed windpipe. I tried, but couldn't push any words out of my mouth.

Then, Macka disappeared as the Berserker within him launched a mighty boot into my side. I yowled and heard my ribs crack as something ruptured and a sickening, burning pain enveloped my entire body. In the corner of my eye, I saw his leg swinging back for another kick, and I prepared to die like a pulpy piñata.

Instead, my old friend raged and stepped over me to smash his head on the cold metal bars.

"Get out!" Macka roared as he fought a hard, internal battle against the animal presence inside him.

Lame, I pulled myself across the floor. I tasted my own blood in my mouth, and breathing was a brutal torture all in itself, but I still managed to get across that floor and out of the cage. Macka smashed his face to a pulp against the bars; blood poured from his head, shards of protruding skull shimmered through his ragged flesh, and his left eye had fallen from its socket to dangle against his smashed jaw.

Using every ounce of my strength, I locked the cage door behind me. Sobbing in pain, tears and snot flowing down my face, I tried to block out the sounds of Macka killing himself as he threw himself again and again at the bars: bones crunched and cracked, muscles and ligaments snapped.

I looked out beyond the cage now, and remembered Charlie and the other Berserkers, but there was no more movement outside of the pen—just a stinking cesspool of ripped flesh, blood, and gore.

Still no explosion.

Chapter Thirteen

Charlie sat across the way, picking out pieces of meat and bone from between his teeth. He was covered head to toe with so much Berserker blood; it was impossible to tell if any of it was his. Then I saw the contrasting slash of blue-grey oozing from the alien's left arm.

"Just fucking explode already," I muttered to myself.

Charlie glanced back at me with surprise burning in those freaky, almost-human eyes. He snarled viciously at me. Once again, a symphony of chirps, whistles, and tweets echoed in my mind. Shaking my head like a dog, I tried to silence them.

"Come and get me, you bastard!" I shouted. My voice was hoarse with pain and impotent rage as I prayed for death to come fast. Charlie ignored me, which filled me with a fury the likes of which I'd never experienced before. "Don't you realize we're both going to get our asses blown to shit, *motherfucker*?" I followed it with the sound effects of an explosion, and strained laughter.

Charlie ignored me and stood up, his muscles rippling like a panther ready to strike. He stretched as if he'd just awoken from a long, refreshing nap, and then headed over to the exit door. Charlie assessed me and peeled his lips back from his teeth in some semblance of a smile. I couldn't process my thoughts rationally— maybe the building had already blown up, and I was in some Charlie-specific hell?

There was the door—the only way out, but with Charlie the blood-thirsty alien standing in front of it smiling at me like some grotesque Boan's greeter.

If we weren't already dead, obviously Charlie wouldn't feel compelled to finish me off. So I reckoned I'd go to him. I struggled to my feet, the room spun, and I face-planted into the floor and slipped into the black abyss.

Noise and motion began to invade my sweet oblivion...

Something was smacking my head as a tight band twisted around my stomach. Above the noise of the sirens I heard a crunch close to my ear. Sparks spewed and lit up my eyelids in soft peaches and pinks. The smell of the beast I'd hidden beneath earlier clung to me, but the stink of an electrical fire was enough to startle me back to consciousness.

Gasping for air, I lifted my head. All I could see was the ground plunging towards me and then cleaving away. Once again, my head smacked against something that was firm but soft. My eyes opened enough to register the long muscular legs beneath me.

Holy shit!

Charlie dropped me on the concrete like a

sack of old spuds. Paralysing fear crippled me. Looking around, I noticed we were back in the room with the vehicles and armoury. The red light from the warning beacons flashed, tendrils of red fingers trying to push back the shadows in that enormous space.

We were at the top of the ramp, which had been lowered to ground level to leave us six feet below the massive door. Charlie hoisted himself up to door level with ease. I heard loud, clanking bangs—what I imagined to be Charlie destroying the mechanical locks on the door. I heard a grunt of exertion and then the rumble of metal as the door started sliding upwards.

Sunlight spilled onto the ramp and dazzled my eyes.

Charlie landed next to me without a noise. I tried to back away. I couldn't imagine—didn't want to imagine—what he wanted with me; I kinda hoped it would be getting blown up together.

Growling in annoyance, he pursed his lips, picked me up, and threw me onto the wall above. My body rolled until I lay half under the door. With a resentful groan, the heavy metal door started moving back down towards me. Charlie's claws tore into my shoulder as he yanked me free just in time.

Then I lost myself to the darkness once again.

Chapter Fourteen

Like slivers of dreams, I sensed rapid movement, like a Jeep racing through the jungle, bouncing L and shuddering. Shafts of light—natural light—peeled away at the edges of my eyes. My sides burned like fire, and enormous rolling waves of pain sent me back to the darkness.

My eyes slid open again. I struggled to breathe, and the pressure in my chest was excruciating and tight. My head felt woozy, and fuzzy white clouds obscured my vision.

I realised I was back in the jungle, slung over Charlie's broad, muscular shoulder.

Behind us, the vibration of a thunderous explosion rocked through my bones as a blinding white heat enveloped the jungle. Charlie cradled me in his arms, protecting me with his immense body. The alien roared in pain as he absorbed the concussion of the blast and the heat which was quick on its tail; I couldn't understand why he was protecting me.

It rained the only way it knew how to rain in that hellish place: large, monsoonal raindrops, fat and tepid to the touch. Oh, but the air was so wonderfully fresh. I wanted to breathe it in deeply and savour its sweetness, but the atmosphere was too thin and the crushing

162

pressure in my chest forced me to sip in small wheezing gasps. I managed to catch a few raindrops on my tongue to quench my thirst before slipping back into the darkness.

Eventually, the light filtered through and, with my throat drier than a dingo's dick, I woke up. I wasn't sure I'd be able to continue to hide in the dreamless sleep I had been so blessed with; I wasn't even sure how long I'd been sliding in and out of consciousness—I'd hoped to have put weeks between me and the insanity I'd witnessed in the bunker, but a quick mental assessment of my body told me it was only hours at best.

In spite of the heat, ice settled into my bones as I found myself laid out on a thick pad of foliage. The incessant buzzing of circling insects imitated the soft flutter of my heart.

I was dying. I waited for death, my vision blurred by a growing grey-black tunnel. I couldn't even find the energy to panic when I saw the thin tube of bamboo protruding from my chest, but then I realised the suffocating pressure in my chest was gone. It didn't take long for me to do the math, yet I couldn't be certain who my medic had been. It didn't matter—I was still dying.

There was no sign of Charlie. There was no sign of anything other than the never-ending green hell that held me tight in its embrace.

After what seemed like an eternity, sounds of

breaking branches and the trampling of plants broke me out of my reverie. And there stood Charlie. He watched me as his large claws retracted to be replaced by soft, padded digits which poked and pushed at the bamboo in my chest.

Instinctively, I tried to move away, to protect myself, but he snarled a warning at me. I saw an innate curiosity in those blue-white eyes of his, and nothing of the fierce beast that had attacked my platoon in the jungle, nor the Berserkers down in the bunker.

Charlie lifted a thin sliver of bamboo, both ends of which had been sharpened to a fine point. With surprising gentleness he stretched out my arm.

Weak as a kitten, I watched him assess my arm before shoving one end of the bamboo straight into my artery. Before I could even think to react, Charlie inserted the other end into a small, deep cut in his forearm. I yelped and tried to move away. A soft, rumbling snarl peeled from between his lips, and he looked at me with firmness in his eyes. I froze.

Then, an icy rush flooded my system. I thought of the Berserkers and panicked, fighting against the alien's intentions. No fucking way did I want to become one of those bastards... No more than I already was.

Icy prickles sliced through my bloodstream, and along with them came an express train of vivid images and memories that fired through my brain.

Chapter Fifteen

My vision was bleary as I opened my eyes. The dust was thick and choked the air. The purple M sky caught my attention; I yearned to stare at it a little longer as it was quite beautiful, but I had no control over my body and my head was wrenched back down to look at my wrist—only it wasn't my wrist, it was Charlie's. A small metal pane lit up there with a combination of symbols I didn't recognise.

"Commander!" A voice echoed deep in my mind. I couldn't answer, but Charlie replied telepathically.

"I'm at the designated RV. Ready to initiate extraction in 90 glodoons."

"The Arc will be in place as arranged... Be careful, Ezeljah, she will not be alone—and she will not come without a fight."

I felt Charlie—his real name was Ezeljah!—twitch as feelings of sadness and regret rolled through him, through *us*. Lifting a huge, double-barrelled, matt black gun with ease, he rolled his shoulders and sighed. With a swipe of his hands, another panel of icons lit up along the gun's length and it emitted a buzzing noise.

"Just be there, Lieutenant."

"Affirmative, sir. Killing communications until you call for the Arc. Over."

Holy shit, I'm reliving Charlie's memories. No, his name is Ezeljah. These are Ezeljah's memories.

Ezeljah stood up straight and strode along the edge of the concrete type wall. His eyes moved steadily, but I recognised the wreckage and ruins, the choking dust and stink of terror that permeated the air.

It's war.

Another time, another place, but still the same shitty signature. It looked like we were in the streets of a city.

Towering buildings, cracking or crumbling, loomed over us, blotting out the sky. Shards of opaque glass lay on the ground, glistening, littering the street along with the rubble from the buildings and broken, wrecked vehicles of sorts that billowed smoke.

This was once a beautiful city; I could tell by the lines and symmetry. Now, however, it was a war zone.

Ezeljah paused at the corner. He checked his weapon and lifted it in silence with one hand on a grip halfway down the shaft, the other on the base. It was a powerful weapon—I sensed the energy pulsing from it. I felt the rush of adrenaline as it flooded through his body, yet I couldn't tell what he was thinking. He rolled around the corner, and his eyes scanned the street that was as lifeless as the one he'd just left. He darted across the street so fast, I didn't realise we'd moved at all.

167

Ezeljah slunk down the side of the building, hiding in its shadow. A tinkle of broken glass broke the silence and Ezeljah spun on his heels. His eyes zoomed in on a shadow in the remains of a first-floor window across the street. His eyes, like Taz's SLR camera, brought the shadow into sharp focus despite the distance.

It looked like Betty.

The thing appeared young, out of proportion, and was mostly certainly a juvenile. It did not see Ezeljah in the shadows. Ezeljah raised his weapon effortlessly, slid his thumb over the control panel and, with a soft hiss, a dart flew across the street and struck the young creature in the neck. It fell to the floor with a gasp, and rolled out of Ezeljah's sight.

Slipping into a doorway, I could hear Ezeljah's two hearts pounding double time. *Jesus, Mary Mother of Christ, two fucking hearts!* He cleared the empty doorway. This place was familiar to him, but once again, I didn't know for sure, it was just a *sense*. This whole thing was just so bizarre; watching things unfold through his eyes, feeling what he felt, and riding his emotions. I knew he was showing me this for a reason, but damned if I knew what that could be.

He crossed through two rooms decorated in bland, minimalist style and stripped of anything of value. I could tell it had been empty for months. The floor was some type of white marble, which shimmered under Ezeljah's feet. It must have been valuable, as I could see where large squares had been cut out and removed.

Looking down, I realised the claws on Ezeljah's feet had retracted into the top of his long, reptilian toes—I guessed to render him soundless sliding on the hard floor. Rapidly, he ascended two flights of stairs; everything was happening so fast—too fast.

We entered into another empty room, this one gutted and with ugly scars on its walls. In front of us was a large, smashed floor-to-ceiling window—the wind blew through it. Ezeljah breathed in the air and it scorched his brain with information. Even I recognised her scent, and I knew I'd know her when I saw her. Anger, sadness, and frustration rippled through Ezeljah; he took in another deep breath to calm his racing emotions.

Peeking his head out of the window for a visual clearance, his eyes locked onto a rooftop across the street. *No fucking way! It must be almost twenty meters away... and down a floor!*

He slung the weapon across his back and strode to the end of the room.

"Target has been located. Ensure Arc is at RV to move." Ezeljah communicated telepathically to his superior officer.

"Arc is moving to location now," the voice replied in his thoughts.

Before I could think, Ezeljah propelled himself across the room at a phenomenal rate. His claws

169

released at his final step to bite into the concrete window frame, and his muscles quivered and tightened to launch us out through the window and across the street. He landed into a roll with a thud onto the rooftop, and we rolled off the edge of the other side. Ezeljah grabbed onto the roof and swung himself through the broken window and into the room below.

Holy fucking shit!

The world had barely stopped spinning before Ezeljah unslung his weapon and aimed it at two beasts standing guard in the room, who looked equally as tall and mean as Ezeljah.

The first one caught the purple light emitted from Ezeljah's weapon with a *fffft* sound. With no time to even open his mouth, the creature's face crumpled to ash and its body collapsed to the floor. Its partner had time to fire a shot off towards us, but Ezeljah jumped, spun high in the air to avoid the shot, and returned one of his own. It struck the second creature in the leg, and it fell as the limb burst into a cloud of dust. Hissing, it tried to regain his balance and fire off another shot, but Ezeljah strode over and kicked the weapon out of his hand with a low growl.

Rage, not fear, grew in the face of the creature with black, beady eyes like tiny slicks of oil. It peeled back its paper thin, purple lips to reveal a set of needle-sharp teeth and a blue forked tongue. It tried to call out, but Ezeljah picked it up by the throat with a single hand and snapped his neck with a deft twist. Revulsion shuddered through Ezeljah as he observed the dead creatures before him; these creatures were evidently as abhorrent to him as they were to me.

Pointing his weapon at the door, Ezeljah's thumb slid over the panel ponce more and a shockwave of energy was released. The door blew in on itself, and lay buckled and twisted in the hallway beyond.

Ezeljah didn't hesitate as he charged through the door and out into the hall. We soon passed a door constructed of thick metal bars. Inside, we heard the rumbles and growls of creatures beyond. With grim resolve, Ezeljah removed several small spheres from somewhere about his person, activated them with the pad of his finger, and tossed them into the room.

Colossal explosions followed us down the hallway as Ezeljah barrelled down its length to leave behind the carnage he'd created. I felt emotion roll over him as her scent grew stronger with every step; his twin hearts were pounding even harder.

Suddenly, an arm as thick as a small tree punched out from the shadow of a doorway. It landed a glancing blow to Ezeljah's nose. Twisting away, eyes watering with pain, Ezeljah slid his weapon underneath his body, and fired blindly at his assailant.

He smelled the ash and knew he had hit his

mark.

Pausing, he breathed deeply and tried to push away the emotional anger, betrayal, and grief that had begun to blind him. He then continued on, and moments later, he charged through the final door, with his weapon blasting as he saw her hidden behind her bodyguards.

Realising she was in danger, she lowered herself to the floor, towards her escape chute, but Ezeljah leapt into the air and over the top of her guards. Landing with a massive thump beside her, he gripped her shoulder and pulled her away from the escape chute.

He threw her into the wall.

The five guards were much the same as the hideous creatures he'd encountered in the first room. Without room to fire, Ezeljah rammed the end of his weapon into the face of one of the creatures, and then turned quickly to the rest, claws extended. Raking out wildly with his razor claws, Ezeljah tore off the face of the creature nearest to him—it fell whimpering to the ground.

Punching hard into the windpipe of the third, Ezeljah flipped him over his knee. The snap of the thing's back resounded like a whip-crack around the room. The fourth, much smaller than the rest, grabbed his arm and dug its small teeth into Ezeljah's skin. Ezeljah shook it like a terrier with a rat until the guard's body flew loose and smacked into the wall with a dull thud.

A loud wail broke out across the room. The

young female Ezeljah had pulled out of the escape chute gathered herself and clambered over to the smallest body.

Ezeljah didn't have time to watch, though, as he had the back of the fifth guard's neck in the vice-like grip of one hand, while with the opposite he dug deep inside the guard's quivering body. With a powerful yank, Ezeljah pulled out the guard's stomach and intestines, which slopped onto the floor in a pile of steaming dark blue.

Panting with exertion, Ezeljah finally looked up to see the young female cradling the small guard's body in her arms. Her ice-blue eyes, filled with hate and revulsion, met his before she looked back down and pulled the broken body closer to her.

"Applauche of the Cafete—you have been summoned to the Triple Council for Justice to answer for your crimes," Ezeljah spoke to her with his mind.

Applauche's head snapped up. Her eyes narrowed and she replied, "And Commander Ezeljah, what crimes will you answer to?" She snarled at him through her teeth.

Ezeljah's shoulders slumped. Not through regret or sadness, it was pure heartbreak that leeched the energy from his body. "I am guilty of no crimes other than falling in love with a spy," he said. "A spy who brought about the destruction of my city, with information she stole from me."

"So, they sent you because we are bonded, and you cannot kill me. Is that right?" She got to her feet, all the while cradling the broken body in her arms.

A rapid, tremendous roar of rushing air closed in over them.

"Commander, the Arc is in place. Prepare to restrain the target for extraction," the voice entered Ezeljah's mind. Moments later, the building shuddered as the roof and the floors above us disappeared in a cloud of fine ash. A rectangular frame, like a stretcher, dropped through the roof to where Ezeljah stood. He grabbed it.

"I came to reclaim some of the honour you stole from me," Ezeljah thought as he walked towards Applauche with the frame vibrating in his hands. She stepped towards him, her eyes burning into him as she offered the broken body in her arms.

"Where is the honour in killing your son?" she hissed as purple tears ran down her cheeks. She stepped into the metal frame.

Confusion, grief, and realisation crashed through Ezeljah to jar his senses numb. He watched as Applauche and his child disappeared into the metal frame he was holding. In an instant, they were frozen in place, her face bereft and grieving, the child—their child—limp with death.

Chapter Sixteen

Something in my brain squealed and thumped as the flicker of images and memories came to a sudden stop. My mind throbbed with the violence of what I'd seen as I tried to process and make sense of it all.

Ezeljah had shown me his past for a reason, of that I was doubly certain...

Slivers of ice scoured my blood, my stomach cramped, and my skin burned as it bulged tight. I longed to tear out my eyes as they stung with the onslaught of colour and brightness, which spun in and out of focus until a wrenching, agonising explosion of noise distracted me.

I was in so much pain I wanted to die, but I couldn't hold that thought as waves of anger, lust, joy, and hatred seared my brain and overwhelmed everything else. My joints and bones throbbed as ligaments tore and ruptured, before knitting themselves back together again in a battle of ice and fire. The world around me swirled in and out as I rocked on the precipice between unconsciousness and hyper-awareness.

Eventually, I gave up fighting it. I lay there numb, feeling every inch of my body being torn down and rebuilt.

I was a fucking Berserker. Fuck this.

Charlie sat beside me with the ease of a

farmer with his toothpick, picking at his gnarly teeth with a shard of bamboo.

"What the hell have you done to me, you bastard?" I mumbled as I came back to full consciousness. I actually *knew* exactly what he'd done to me—he'd made me one of those hellish abominations. I hated him for that, and if my body hadn't felt like it was stuck in a patch of wet concrete, I would have killed him there and then with my own bare hands.

Charlie shrugged his shoulders as if he'd heard me, and that riled me even more.

"Yeah laugh, you son of a bitch. I'll send you back to where you came from." My knotted throat squeezed out the threat. I wilfully ignored the fact he'd just saved my life. What was the point of that if I was to be a savage animal like him? In my book, he was no better than Harding and her sick experiments. Grimacing, I tentatively stretched out my cramped, knotted arms and legs, and rolled onto my side.

"*Motherfucker!*" I grunted as I saw Charlie look at me with amusement dancing in those ice-blue eyes.

"Yes, you, Charlie—or whatever the fuck your name is. You should have killed me."

A melodic humming started up inside my head. It was a familiar chorus of chirps and whistles, which cracked and shattered into words. "Ezeljah. Call me Ezeljah. I do not ever want to hear the name *Charlie* again."

176

I gasped as Charlie/Ezeljah turned to look at me and his eyes burned into my soul.

"Yes, you are *thinking* my words. Ectron, my people, no longer use verbal language. It is not efficient."

"Get, out of my head! I don't want you in my head!"

I screamed.

Ezeljah jumped to his feet and snarled. "I did what I had to, to save your life. You humans are delicate, but you fix easily too." He pointed at the bamboo pipe sticking out of my chest. Images of the crazed Berserkers flooded my mind and sweat ran down my back as I wondered when my change would begin—if it had not already.

Ezeljah looked at me and made a coughing noise in his chest. Sparks of laughter filled my mind. "Those animals are Applauche's accidents. She has no idea of what she's doing."

And you do? I thought quietly to myself—or so I thought.

"More than Applauche."

Numbness punched me hard in the chest as I realised why those Applauche's eyes looked so familiar, and why I'd recognised her scent.

"Your wife is Harding?" I asked.

Ezeljah avoided my eyes and looked away. "Yes, and you must kill her."

The thought came to me so quietly I almost missed it.

Almost. Exhausted, I closed my eyes. I was a

physical and mental wreck; it was like my mind had been thrown about in a hurricane.

I couldn't catch a single coherent thought before I sunk into the blackness.

Chapter Seventeen

I woke up not long past dawn to a soft hum, a vibration of diesel engines in the air, the thick stink of ozone, and Charlie's—no, *Ezeljah's*—firm grip on my arm.

"Be calm. We have time still."

"Time? Five minutes at best! We've got to move, now!" My voice squeaked with panic.

"Calm. They are your people. I have been listening to their approach for a while now. They won't make it before the rain, though. We are at the extraction point you arranged prior to being captured: with Bravo 2

Alpha. We should move towards them."

"Extraction point, how the hell do you know about that?"

"You saw my memories, and I saw yours. It's all part of the transfer. I have also removed the tube from your chest. Your lung has healed and should prove adequate.

Do be aware that my lungs do not work as effectively in this atmosphere as yours do..."

Instinctively, my hand clutched at my chest. There was no pipe, just a little pressure that felt like the asthma that plagued my childhood. Clawing apart the few remaining buttons of my shirt, I gawked at the smooth skin under my fingers. I gasped and stared at Ezeljah. "What the

179

fuck?"

"We have time, but not much. Applauche will find you. Tomorrow or next year, she *will* find you. She will be ruthless once she realises you're still alive. You must find her first and kill her."

"Me? What the hell? I'm not going anywhere near that psychopath. Why don't you sort her out? She is your fucking wife!" I yelled.

"She is… she *was*… my mate. But we are pair bonded and cannot kill each other. You saw that in my memories. Our bonds forbid it. Otherwise, she would have killed me long ago." I winced at his shared pain.

"Well, I'm not going near that bitch. She's a fucking monster." I cautiously stretched and tested my muscles.

I was surprised to find them light and fresh, not in the least plagued with the aches and tears I would have expected, given the last few days.

"You *must*, and I will not leave you until you do. I will help you." Ezeljah was quite vehement.

"I don't want your fucking help. I just want to get the fuck out of here and forget this shit ever happened."

"That will not happen. If you do not find Applauche, she will find you and your family. She will hurt them. It is her way. This is not over until Applauche is dead. I know you are scared."

"No, I'm not fucking scared, because it's not fucking happening. This shit just doesn't happen. Besides, she just left me there to die. She doesn't give a flying fuck about me."

"This is your tracking beacon." Ezeljah held up a tiny sliver of metal between his finger pads. "She will shortly realise you were not caught in the blast. She already knows I survived; Applauche will not want to lose both of us to the Russians."

"So, you helped me to escape so I can kill your wife?"

"I will be with you, but it will be done. For my people and for yours, it must happen. You know what it is to be betrayed by the woman you love."

I snapped my head up and the heavy stink of diesel, metal, and sweaty male bodies filled my nose. For the first time, I noticed how vivid the world had become for me. I no longer saw the jungle as just a mass of green.

My sight focused as sharply as if I was looking through Taz's camera lens. I saw each individual tree, branch, leaf, and the insects hiding on each leaf. It was stunning.

The hum of the Jeep had gotten louder; I could even hear the grind of the gears. I shivered, both amazed and terrified.

"Is it really like this?" I asked Ezeljah. "Everything is so strong."

Ezeljah gave me a curious look. "You humans truly have such poor senses; it amazes me how you survived as a species."

"No natural predators made us kings," I mused.

"Not anymore. Not if Applauche has her way." His eyes burned into mine. "The Carfetes are seeking freedom, on a new planet, and with their ability to mimic other species—or just parts of them, like your lungs for example—Earth would be a perfect habitat for them. They won't be like the Enki and evolve the two species together. They will simply wipe you out entirely or keep you as slaves. The Carfete are dangerous."

A new sound filled the air. The thrum of helicopter blades ripped through the sky. Not close, but coming in faster than the Land Rovers. I looked at Ezeljah, and saw his sinewy muscles taut and ready to flee or fight as he cocked his head in on the sound.

"Not your people. They are the other people. The *Russians* Applauche fears." I sensed panic as his thoughts tumbled through his mind.

"She's scared of the Russians?"

"They—the Russians—have other species that will either stop her Carfete claim on Earth, or destroy the Carfete," he snarled.

Images of a heavy sided, twin rotor bird with six-bladed rotors flicked into my mind. A Russian Yak. I remember the picture of the large helicopter from a science rag I'd picked up in the barracks. It was a mammoth helicopter; I couldn't mistake it. It had only meant to be a prototype, some kind of Russian fantasy sci-fi.

"Russians," I said. "Harding, I mean *Applauche*, said it was the Russians that had found us. It's why she blew up the lab. Why'd she destroy everything?"

"Not *everything*," Ezeljah sighed. "Go that way towards your people. I will lead these Russians away. You must find Applauche and kill her. You owe me."

"I owe you Jack shit. You turned me into this *thing*...

I don't even know what the fuck I am right now.

Besides, she took off and is probably miles away by now," I said.

Ezeljah shook his head slowly. "No, she will stay close to keep an eye on any loose ends. I know her well.

I did not change you, Applauche already started the process. I merely finished it to save your life. This is all bigger than you and I. You must do this."

The bird was coming in fast. I could see it in the distance, punching through the horizon as the *wokka wokka* of the double rotors turned deafening. I felt small and vulnerable, like a mouse in an open field with a hungry eagle circling. Panic rippled through my body.

"Jesus Christ, it knows exactly where we are," I mumbled.

"They have a tracker on board. Run. Now— toward your vehicles!"

"What about you? You said you'd stay with me until it's done." I knew the answer before the words fell out of my mouth.

Ezeljah shrugged, tapped my head and my heart, and said, "I will be with you until this ends. This place or that place; I will be with you." He leapt away, tearing through the jungle at a phenomenal rate.

I tried to block out the deafening sound of the Yak to hear the softer whirrs of the Jeeps. I heard the gentle groan and rumbles of the engines and ran off like a madman in their direction while trying to hide amongst the foliage. Explosions rang out to the north of me as the Yak fired missiles into the dense vegetation, straight into Ezeljah's path. The noise was overwhelming, and I quickly found myself disorientated and struggling to locate the sound of the Jeeps.

Gradually the explosions and machine-gun fire died away into the distance as I made good ground.

"Run." Ezeljah's voice vibrated in my brain; there came a blast of pain, and it went black.

I snapped back into myself and stood up. Trying to shake off the vision, I was dizzy and trembling, but I pushed myself forward. The Jeeps had stopped because of the helicopter attack, but I was close enough to smell the diesel, metal, and sweat.

Then, the rain broke.

A typical 'Nam shower—a thick deluge that brought visibility down to a minimum—tore the earth into bog holes of mud and washed away

184

the scent the Jeeps. The sound of the rain alone took me down to my knees. I clutched at my ears and screamed with the pain of it all.

Gradually the pain eased, or I'd become simply numb to it, and I clambered back to my feet. I sucked the humid air in through my nose. The band around my chest tightened as I found the Jeeps again. There they were, but so was something else...

An explosion of gunfire broke out through the curtain of rain in the direction of the vehicles. I didn't think twice before I ran off toward it. I'd always been a fast runner, but now my legs stretched out at such a rapid pace that I fell to the ground a few times, as I was so unused to such momentum. Something acrid and bitter permeated the air, the sour stench of death and fear. It made me hesitate, but then I heard an Aussie voice call out in battle rage. I answered in a blood-curdling roar that scared the shit out of me.

The rain stopped just as I came down from above the road where the convoy had been ambushed. Out of the convoy of five, both the front and rear vehicles lay twisted on their sides and smoking despite the rain.

Several bodies lay broken, ripped, and torn around the burning wreckages. One was trapped within the wreckage—I *heard* his pulse flicker and falter, then stop. I thought with anguish, *The Aussie soldiers came to bring me home.* Rage boiled inside me; they hadn't been shot, they'd been slaughtered.

I froze when I saw Harding/Applauche dragging a flailing, bloodied soldier out of the back of a Jeep. The soldier hung onto the rear towbar with grim determination. I heard his shoulder pop and he pulsed with pain as the alien bitch dragged him around the jungle floor. Applauche's skin, glistening a ghostly grey, was streaked with rivers of bright blood and rain; she flared her nostrils and sniffed at the air until she looked directly at me. Her eyes bore straight into mine, and I saw a momentary look of shock, pleasure, and lust flicker across her features.

She released the soldier's leg.

A tickle of fingers traced across my brain, but I pushed it away fast.

Applauche smiled, and my gut turned to ice as she morphed back into the shape of Jacinta Harding. Stark naked and so fucking sexy it hurt just to look at her.

What the fuck was she doing there? She should have been far away by now.

"I'm pleased to see you're alive," Harding said with her trademark smile.

"Yeah, no thanks to you, bitch," I responded. The heat of my anger thawed that icy feeling in my gut in an instant.

"You reek of Ezeljah. He changed you, didn't he? I know he's still alive. Is he still with you?" she asked.

Her nostrils flared wide and she sniffed the air again.

"Maybe," I answered. "What are you doing here?

Shouldn't you be busy running away?" I surveyed the slaughter around me.

"Oh, we were, and then we saw your tracker come up on the radar."

"My tracker?" I tried to play dumb.

"Yes. Everybody at the lab was fitted with a tracking device. You're far too valuable to be left to the Russians, and we last saw your tracker heading in this direction before the signal went dead. Ezeljah must have removed it at some point. I remembered the extraction point Private Jacobs mentioned, and thought it was worth a shot."

"You told them I was dead. They shouldn't have been here. Why did you do this to them?" My anger rose in a white haze as my fingers found a two-inch scar line on the back of my neck where Ezeljah had removed the tracking device.

"I never told them you were dead. Originally, I was hoping they would send me more useful samples like you, but no. These are all very ordinary. And now they are loose ends. It's been fun, but now you're here..."

Taking advantage of her distraction, the soldier at Harding's feet rolled over and jammed his pocketknife in her foot and scrambled to get away. She hissed in pain and bent over to remove the blade. She waited until the soldier got to his feet before pouncing. She didn't take her eyes off me for a single second.

She knocked the soldier back down into the mud and straddled his body with her with teeth snapping at his face. Placing one foot on his chest, flickering between Applauche and Harding, she eased her weight onto his chest as her eyes locked onto mine.

I heard the soldier's ribs crack. I shouted at her to stop, and my body snapped and pinged with adrenaline.

The soldier's face convulsed in pain, and I launched myself at her.

Applauche was expecting me, and we met in mid-air.

My momentum sent us rolling into the mud. Grunting with the impact, she flickered into Harding. I hesitated as that beautiful, naked body lay writhing under mine—not to escape but to excite. Pheromones exploded in the air like a cloud of perfume to scramble my senses. She was good, but I knew better. I pulled my fist back and smashed it into her delicate jaw with all my weight behind it.

A satisfying crack rang out. My arm jarred, and I straddled her as she flickered into Applauche once again. Her lust turned to rage and she released a shrill screech that made my eardrums ache. She threw me off before I could land more than a glancing blow—her strength surprised me. I landed, winded, in the mud and twisted out of her way just as she raked her claws down towards my head.

The world floated around me, and dark spots clouded my eyes as Harding's other fist followed through and connected with my temple. My body turned to jelly as she somersaulted onto her feet to stand over me.

My brain screamed at my body to do something, *anything*, but there was no reaction—it was like trying to start a car with a flat battery. The crushing pressure of Applauche's foot on my chest was the connective spark my body needed. I grabbed her foot, lifted it up with strength I didn't know I possessed, pulled it forward over my shoulder, and kicked at her other leg to throw her off balance.

Blindly, I swung my arm, and was lucky to connect with the inside of her knee. It snapped it out sideways and Applauche lost balance in the slippery mud; she fell, crouched over my chest and shoulders. Lifting herself up, Applauche pinned my arms down into the mud, pushing down on me with all her weight. The rings of teeth that filled her crotch stretched and gaped as she tilted her pelvis towards my face.

Holy Mother Of God!

I tried to wriggle out from underneath Applauche, my arms flailing against her weight as she lowered that vicious maw down towards my face. I turned my head away from the multitudes of barbed teeth that waved and trembled, and the foul odour of sex, fish, and rotten meat pervaded my senses. I choked on the bile that burned the back of my throat; I could feel the heat of her sex as it kissed my skin.

Inspiration hit me—self-defence 101: *the attacker's balance and force will be concentrated on you resisting in direct oppositional force.* Changing my tactic, I instead of pushing back against Applauche with my arms. I slid them out wide in the mud to unbalance her. As all her strength had been focused down, she didn't have time to adjust her balance and toppled forward. With a last desperate push, I managed to slide out from beneath her. A few of those God-awful teeth slid across my scalp as I escaped and scrabbled to my feet. She stood there, hissing at me.

"You are one sick fucking bitch," I said.

She threw herself at me again. This time, I pulled her down with me and managed to kick her off using all my strength. Flying backward, Applauche landed with a heavy thud as her head connected with the door of one of the Jeeps.

It was only then I noticed the now familiar, elongated claws curled in front of my face.

They were mine.

My skin had a grey hue, my body was thick with muscle, and I was tall like Ezeljah. The hood of the Jeep, which had previously come up to my torso, was now in line with my hip. I was Ezeljah, yet still very much me . A flicker in my peripheral vision brought me back into the fight, as Applauche struggled to her feet and charged towards me with a hellish snarl. Her body was in an uncoordinated frenzy, and it dawned on me she was not a natural fighter—I might've had half a chance...

At the very last moment, I stepped to the side and grabbed the thick cords that hung hanging from her head like dreadlocks. I wrenched her head down and backward, but I didn't see the wheel jack in her hand.

She swung it over her body and it connected with the side of my skull. The sensation of being clipped lightly on the head reminded me of how my father used to punish me; lights flashed behind my eyes, but I kept my grip on her hair.

"Your father, I will find him and kill him. Along with your she-bitch Jenny," Applauche snarled as she fought and scrambled in the mud, unable to find traction. Foam splattered from around her thin, blue lips. Rows of sharp, tiny teeth mirrored those rooted in her cunt—she was a vile, disgusting creature.

A roar of anger escaped my throat, as I looked down on the face that had killed and tortured so many; I could never let her get near my family. I twisted the wheel jack out of her hand, threw it away over my shoulder, and hammer-fisted her fucking face.

Applauche roared as I reached back again and

rammed my fist into her stomach. She curled into a tight ball. I wrenched her head back up and straight, and glared at that face, a face I knew would haunt me for the rest of my life. Applauche swiftly morphed into Harding, and in an instant her sumptuous, naked body was writhing against me as she seduced me with those powder blue eyes and that mouth.

Oh, God, that mouth…

My grip loosened a little as Harding took on the mantle of a woman in need of saving. *Are men so truly hardwired for a damsel in distress it stupefies our common sense?*

But, instead of desire, my fury peaked. I wrapped Harding's long, golden tresses of hair in my beast's hand, and I brought my fist down with rage onto her face, again and again as she slumped towards unconsciousness.

Instinct lowered my mouth to her throat; I was ready to tear it apart. I sensed the blood pumping through her arteries, thick and ice cold. I began to salivate as savage desire overtook me.

And before I could stop myself, I'd ripped into the delicate flesh of her throat. Dark blue blood sprayed over us both as it pulsed from her body with each heartbeat. Bitterness exploded down my throat as Harding's body fell lifeless and limp, and I dropped her on the wet ground. As she fell, the large, jagged hole in her throat yawned open like a wide, smiling mouth and gurgled with blood.

I expected to feel some kind of triumphant, vindicated, powerful, justice shit. This woman, this *creature* who'd tortured and murdered my mates along with God only knew how many more had died just like everybody else in this fucked up place: brutally and alone.

Still, it fell far short of the justice she'd deserved. Of course, it all was too easy, and I didn't move fast enough when I heard the wooden rifle stock swinging towards me from behind.

The last thing I remember was the sound of Sergeant Boots Bodean Perry roaring with wrath.

Chapter Eighteen

I found myself slumped against a tree stump at the top of a muddy embankment. I had no gun, not even a fucking rock to defend myself. My vision was bleary and out of focus and nausea rolled through my stomach.

And there was Boots, his back facing me. In the distance, I could hear the American Huey closing in, but we had at least five minutes yet. I recovered fast from the blow, but not fast enough. Before I knew it, ass-face Boots Bodean Perry was looking me in the eye. Yeah, he was one angry looking mother-fucker.

"He turned you, didn't he?" he snarled. He walked over to me. "I can smell it; you stink worse than a filthy fucking nigga. You reek of him—makes me fucking sick. They can only share their essence with one person, and he fucking chose a yellow tar baby. He made you kill her, and now he's going to..."

"She got everything she fucking deserved, the psycho bitch!" I spat out a large wad of bloodied phlegm in Boots' direction.

In a show of strength, Boots pulled me up from the ground, his fingers digging deep in my shoulders. My blood rush had gone, my limbs were jelly—I would've fallen over if he hadn't been holding me up. My senses were still super sharp, or maybe he just *really* stank, but waves of beer, chewing tobacco, and her... he reeked of *her*.

"She chose a fucking dumb-ass, red-neck yank," I sneered as the realisation dawned on me. Boots' face flushed red as he drew back his fist and rammed it into my guts so hard that my feet left the floor. I dropped like a stone; I couldn't breathe, and with my diaphragm trying to claw its way back out of my throat, I could only watch helplessly as a size ten G.I boot sailed into the side of my head. Stars shot like fireworks inside my brain, and I blacked out for a few seconds.

My eyes slid open. My swift recovery, while not great, proved to me that Ezeljah still lingered in my blood.

Boots had his back to me as he looked for the Huey; the chopper's blades thumped louder now, even amongst the more solid *whoomp-whoomp* of the Russian Yaks that still hovered above the area. The sheer volume of the noise was debilitating, but I knew there was a way I could block it out and focus as I'd done while trying to locate the Jeeps. With my brain jellied, it was beyond me. I prayed for Boots' lack of attention to continue. Of course, there was no such luck...

Boots threw a green smoke grenade in the clearing near the wrecked Jeeps and then strode purposefully towards me.

"Why don't you just kill me?" I snarled.

Boots knelt close to me and answered, "Trust me, I want to tear you apart, piece by piece."

"Go on then, be done with it."

"I don't know where Dr. Harding put the briefcase.

So, now *you're* my briefcase—a living petri-fucking-dish, an insurance policy. You're mine, and once they are done with you, I'll make sure I'm there to take out the trash."

"So, you're in it for the money?" I tried to think how I could buy myself more time, time enough to recover.

"Why do you hate me so much, man?"

Boots spat out a wad of tobacco phlegm and gazed over to the horizon where a black dot in the distance grew larger.

"I don't hate ya'll," he finally responded. "Fuck, nigga, ya'll ain't worth the fucking energy for hating on."

"Well, why have you gotta call me nigga and shit, man? That isn't nice, you know." My world started to come back into focus.

"Cos you is a nigga. I don't care where ya'll from.

You're all black bastard jungle monkeys to me," he said, his eyes peeled to the sky.

"I may be black, but you've killed your own bloody mates, your own countrymen, and allies. What the hell does that make you?"

"I never killed nuthin' that weren't already killing itself." He continued his vigil.

196

"That's bullshit, man. Them blokes, they came fighting for your country. Your country called them."

"Arghh! They ain't nothing but white trash. Little better than you niggas. They are fools, is what they are.

Think they can come out here and get some name for 'emselves. Fucking fools. They think someone gives a fuck. The only person gettin' anything out of this fucking war is me and anyone that owns a fucking munitions factory." I never realised Boots was such a talker. Now, I wish I hadn't started him off.

I estimated the Huey was only a minute away at best.

I guessed it could have taken up to five minutes to touch it down in this tight area. Nah, they'd hover, but even that would take time to get into the right speed and position. Then, they would have to winch out the ropes to haul us up. Yeah, I had at least five minutes. I remembered the last time I had five minutes—it didn't end so well.

Energy burned through my veins once more, and I caught the whiff of adrenaline seeping from my pores.

Boots' nose was upwind and I hoped he wouldn't smell it.

I looked around again for a weapon of any sort, but I only had whatever-the-fuck I had on my body—I was my own weapon. The bird swooped in low, shaking the crap out the trees with the updraft from its blades. It zoomed off to swing around again, closing its circle with each pass. Boots stepped back towards me. He stood just two metres away with his back to me. Now was my last chance as the helicopter shot out of sight.

I coiled my body, as slow and silent as possible, and brought my knees up to my chest. I rested there for a few breaths, hoping I appeared harmless enough as I tried to gauge how my body was responding. I endured the sharp, stinging pull as claws ruptured from my fingertips; I muffled my pained groans into my knees. I jerked backwards and one of my razor-sharp incisors cut into the side of my knee. I tasted my own blood, expecting the all too familiar coppery taste. Instead, there was an acidic bitterness. Still curled over, I rocked onto the balls of my feet and launched myself into the air just as Boots lifted his arm and swung around to face me.

The *pfft* of the 50. caliber tranquiliser gun registered only after the biting sting of the needle found my forearm. *I hadn't been fast enough*, I thought as I drove Boots' body into the ground with a meaty thump. He grunted in pain as the air punched out of his lungs.

Furious, I snatched the tranquiliser dart out of my arm and clenched it in my fist. I didn't know how long it would take to work, or even if it would, but at least now I had a weapon... of sorts. I jammed it into Boots' throat. He reeled, gasping, hands flailing at his neck where the dart jutted out. I don't know if anything of the drug was left in it, or even if it would affect him, but it sure as hell pissed him off.

Boots managed to knock the dart out. I reached for it again, and he saw the window in my attention before punching me in the throat. It was a weak punch, but it did the job; I hung on to him, choking, with stars bursting behind my eyes from lack of oxygen.

I managed to push his head into the churned up muddy floor with one hand; my claws slid deep into his scalp. Boots twisted and wriggled beneath me, moving his head enough until his sharp teeth clamped down hard and tore into my hand like some savage animal. I recoiled, more in shock than pain and, with me still struggling to breathe, Boots landed a flailing, meaty fist on my jaw. Another weak hit, but it came again and again, beating at my head like it was a bass drum in a marching band.

I'm not sure if it was the thumping I was receiving, or the sedative, but I was becoming sluggish. I heard the Huey settling into position above us, and I knew I had to stop fucking around and get away.

Chunks of mud and greenery were hurled around in the air, accompanied by the rattle of the Huey's guns. It took me a moment to recognise they were actually firing at us—well me, specifically.

White-hot pain lanced my shoulder and I fell forward onto my elbow, just enough for Boots to weasel his way out from underneath me, and leave behind a patch of grey, bristly scalp in my hand.

The firing stopped as soon as Boots was free. Blood ran down the fucker's face as he rose unsteadily to his feet. I struggled to stand up on my own, and Boots stepped in with a terrific roar and laid one into my ribs.

The splintered ends of my ribs stabbed into my lungs, and I lay gasping as the world spun out of control.

"I should've fucking killed you, motherfucker,"

Boots grunted as he straddled me and drew both my wrists back together behind my back to bind them with tape. He made quick work of the rest and had me ready in short order. I didn't even put up a fight—I couldn't.

Yes, you should have. Please do, I thought numbly.

Harding's limp body got winched up first, a black silhouette of a five-point star. Her long-corded hair swung around in the air. The careful removal was either an act of loyalty from Boots, or he was cashing in on another of his petri dishes.

It seemed to take forever before Boots jerked on the rope he'd slung around my body. He'd trussed me up like a prized pig ready for the slaughter. It started to rain the moment they started winching us up, with Boots standing on my back like some sort of fucking trophy hunter. I hated trophy hunters—they were usually fat, pompous white guys who called it sport to shoot animals from three hundred meters away with a group of trackers, guides, and scouts to do the dirty work. I had some grudging respect for Boots in retrospect. He did at least take me face-to-face, hand-to-hand. Actually no, *he knocked me out from behind and tranquilised me,* I reminded myself.

It was a typical Nam rain; a deluging curtain in which one could scarcely breathe without drowning. My lungs screamed in agony as I fought to let in as much air as I could. The muddy earth clung to my body, as if not wanting me to leave its hellish embrace. The rain created a veil of opaque grey, which distorted my view as I finally left the green hell behind for good.

Or so I thought...

Chapter Nineteen

A shadow lurched in the corner of my vision. Boots shrieked in anger as a massive weight hit A the ropes. They swung and jarred my body before it was wrenched back towards the earth; my stomach rolled before I punched into the ground like a broken fist. Some foliage had broken my fall, but mostly it was me that was broken. The spit of gunfire broke out around me as the Huey shot at the massive shadow, the Ezeljah-shaped shadow that hung on the end of the ropes.

I lay there, back on the jungle floor, stunned and unable to move, roll, or even moan. I tried to take in the scene above me, but the fat raindrops stung my eyeballs.

Ezeljah was swinging, and then falling, with a large branch in his hand. The branch changed shape and became more familiar as it descended towards me, gripped in Ezeljah's fist.

It was a leg.

Boots' leg.

Where the fuck was the rest of Boots?

Ezeljah landed heavily beside me. I heard the crack of a missile shoot over the top of the Huey. It was then I noticed the sound of the Yaks. The Huey pitched, almost losing control, as it tried to dodge a second incoming missile that barely missed its skid and exploded into the tree canopy nearby.

I saw Boots in silhouette; a swirling, dead weight as the rope around his waist whipped around. Boots' three remaining limbs splayed out, limp, like a ghoulish sacrificial offering as the Huey shot off to the South.

"Thank you... for saving me... again!" I gasped.

Already I felt my body knitting together, healing itself.

Ezeljah glanced at Boots' leg in his hand. He cast it away with a look of disgust upon his face. "I killed her. I killed her like you asked."

"I know. I felt it." His words rumbled into my brain as he walked over to me. With a precise scratch of his mighty claw, he sliced through my restraints; I almost fainted with pain as the circulation hit my arms and legs with full force. The rain stopped. The roar of the Russian Yak was louder—it was closing in.

"Now I must destroy all the evidence. All of her research." Ezeljah's words tumbled into my mind as he breathed in the air, sucking it in through his nose. I pulled my body up into a sitting position and watched him bound off into the jungle.

He returned a few moments later with the large metal briefcase Harding had hidden earlier. He rifled through it, smashing jars, breaking syringes, and tearing up papers and files. I looked away as Ezeljah searched the bodies of the fallen soldiers until he found what he needed. Ezeljah unhooked the F1 grenade, pulled the pin and lobbed it at the briefcase. In a flash and a bang, the remains were destroyed in a shower of paper, smoke, and ash.

"Finally, it's over. We need to get out of here. The Russians are coming," I warned him. I struggled to my feet and limped towards Ezeljah. I saw the look in his eyes at the same time as I noticed the grenade clutched tight to his chest. He appeared regretful, yet resolute.

Fuck, I hated that look.

"No, man, you don't have to do this. No one is going to fucking believe me."

"I am sorry it has to be this way. But, one look at your blood..." He sighed and looked away.

"No fucking way! I didn't do all this, go through *that*, so you can fucking blow me up with a goddamn grenade! No fucking way! You said I could go home!"

The anger flowed through my body. I understood what he meant, it made perfect sense, but I wanted to live. I wanted to survive this hell and get through to the other side. I wanted life more than anything else at that moment. Jenny, yes, I wanted Jenny even if she didn't want me. And, I wanted my son. I would fight for him.

The Yak was getting closer. I had to think fast. Was living as a guinea pig better than dead?

Yes. It was life.

All animals, humans included, have a primal instinct to live, no matter what. Even people committing suicide fight to live, consciously or unconsciously, at the last second. That basic desire, hunger, lust for life is written in our very DNA. So, no, I wasn't going just to lie down and let myself be blown up.

Fuck that shit!

I turned and ran into the jungle. Ezeljah's sigh echoed through my mind; it didn't matter if he wanted to do it or not, he was going to do it for the greater good.

The jungle crashed behind me. I knew I wasn't going to get far, but could I hold on long enough for the Yak to interfere? Branches tore at my face and vines snagged at my feet, and Ezeljah was almost on top of me before I had even started. Still I ran, my heart pounding in my throat as I circled the area, wanting to stay close to where the Yak could find us but deep enough in the jungle where Ezeljah would be slowed down by the dense vegetation. Not by much, but maybe *enough*.

The Yak roared overhead. Holy shit, there were two of them! I turned into the centre where the Jeeps lay, their broken carcasses glinting in the sun. Machine gun fire broke out from the Yaks, spitting lead into the ground around us.

Glancing over my shoulder, I saw Ezeljah pounce just before I broke into the clearing; I dodged to the right to throw him off course.

The earth gave way beneath me. I fell, tumbling into darkness. White-hot pain seared my leg when I landed, and sparks lit up behind my eyes as I hit my head.

Above me, the Yaks opened up and released their full arsenal onto Ezeljah.

Under rocket fire, the ground exploded and shook violently with shockwaves. Between the dust and thick smoke, I caught a glimpse of one of Ezeljah's clawed feet hanging limp over the edge of the trap that had caught me; it disappeared almost as soon as I saw it.

Chunks of mud and debris landed on top of me, and then the wall at the far end collapsed. The thick, cloying earth slid over me like a smothering blanket to pin me to the ground. I couldn't move at all; my leg had been pierced by a long, wooden stake.

I had fallen into a half-finished VC booby trap, and whilst I had evaded both the Russians and Ezeljah, the earth was crushing my lungs and I could only breathe the foul air in ragged, desperate gasps.

A blood-curdling roar, tinged with rage, fear, and pain, echoed through my mind. They'd got him. I *knew* it. The machine gun fire and explosions ceased and the silence was deafening. I only heard the rumble of the Yaks as they continued to hover overhead. The air was clogged with gunfire, smoke, and the thick, ozone reek of a brewing storm. Black dots swam across my vision as I struggled to hang onto consciousness, but I slid in and out of the darkness.

Not long after I heard troops on the ground barking instructions. Ezeljah roared in fury and I still sensed the fight going out of him. A bitter chemical leached from his skin and I guessed they'd tranquilised and trapped him. Just when I thought he had finally given up the fight, his voice echoed through my mind, *"Finish this."*

I pushed the thought away. I had enough on just trying to survive.

I tried to quiet my short gasps as a shadow fell over me. I prayed. I was well enough hidden under the suffocating blanket of earth and debris. I closed my eyes and let my body go limp. If they saw me, I looked dead.

I lost track of how long I lay covered in dirt, my leg speared to the ground, and struggling to breathe, yet it must have been only about thirty minutes before the Russian Yaks started to move off with their cargo.

Still, I waited.

Chapter Twenty

Time passed and when the sun no longer glared down into the pit, I began the laborious process of digging myself out. Despite my alien-aided rapid recovery, progress was still painful and slow. After a concentrated effort, I uncovered the meaty part of my calf at the bottom of a forty-five inch stake. Punji booby traps were awful. Not only did you often break a limb falling in, or die instantly by impalement, but also most of the stakes were covered in shit. So even if a dozen wooden stakes rammed through your body didn't kill you, the infection would give it a damn good go. When it came to booby traps, the VC were vicious bastards.

I found another six stakes whilst digging myself out.

One had spliced my rib cage, leaving a deep and angry cut. The rest, through sheer dumb fucking luck, had missed me, or broken under my fall. I clenched a piece of wood between my teeth when it came time to extract the stake through my leg, and despite my careful preparations, I ended up shattering the wood and ripping the stake out of my leg in a violent rage before blacking out with the pain.

It was about an hour before nightfall when I managed to climb, exhausted out of the pit.

I surveyed the ground around me. The jungle had been torn up under the Russian firepower—not one part in the vicinity had been left unsullied by their attack. This was the ugly shit stain of war. Sympathy overwhelmed me as I thought of Ezeljah, but then again, the bastard had used me and tried to kill me. His final thought kept haunting me: *"Finish this."*

I pushed it away. I had one hundred problems, and that was not one of them. Gingerly, I approached the wreckage of the Jeeps.

Most of the bodies were now covered in a thick deluge of dirt. I collected all the dog tags I could and armed myself as well as I was able to. My dumb luck continued. I managed to flip one of the Jeeps back on its side, and after pumping and bleeding the fuel line, it rumbled into life. I swapped its shredded tyre with one from another wrecked Jeep. Then, after raiding the dead soldiers' ration packs, I devoured two days worth of freeze-dried rations and polished the survival biscuits the lads and I often called 'dog biscuits.' My mood, initially pepped by the Jeep and food, dropped. I curled up in a ball and drifted off into a fitful sleep.

I drove south for two days. I was jumpy and anxious, and it was slow going. Every time I heard the *whoomp, whoomp, whoomp* of a bird in the sky, I would drive as far into the jungle as I could. I enjoyed my new strength as I had to dig and winch my way out of bogs. *"Finish this"* still haunted my every thought and action. But still, I refused to really think about anything other than staying on the road and staying alive.

I smelt civilisation before I could see it. After nothing but diesel and jungle, it was an offensive odour of human waste, food, and the communal living of fear-laced, sweating bodies. It was then that terror overtook me. I pulled the Jeep off the road and into the jungle so I could gather myself. I was so close.

Everything that had happened those last few days hit me with raw emotion as I sat in the Jeep with its engine dead. I cried for my mates, for their brutal, unnecessary deaths. It could easily have been me, except I was protected by my mother's blood. My poor mother, who never even got to hold me, had protected me with the very thing I hated about myself. I rode the waves of anger and frustration of how fucked-up this fucking war was. The depth of the lies and the sheer arrogance of those in power was so frustrating that it tore me up inside. It was already wrong, but this, this made it even worse. I purged myself in that tiny metal cab, the vinyl seat sticking to my sweat-soaked clothes.

I realised then just how totally alone I'd become. I couldn't trust anybody with this— that's if I ever found anyone who'd believe me. I guess I could offer a blood sample, or show them what I could do, what I could *become*. But then what? I would become a lab experiment and sold back to the US?

No, I was alone, so very alone. Despite my dreams of Jenny, I was further from her now than ever before. And our son—I was too fucking dangerous for him now. I had never fit in with being neither white nor black, but now I wasn't even sure if I was *human*. I glanced at the rear-view mirror. My stomach dropped as Ezeljah gazed back at me. My mud-brown eyes were now slivers of icy blue. Would anybody even recognise me?

I had hoped the effects would wear off, be just temporary like the flu. Instead, I felt fresh as a daisy.

The results of being drugged, beaten, hunted, crushed, and shot were all gone. The bullet hole in my shoulder was but a shiny silver scar. The hole in my leg, still pink and angry-looking, but appearing to be about two months old rather than two days.

Fuck. Why me? I had nowhere to run. I couldn't run away from this.

As for Jenny, I didn't care if she was with Simon, as long as she was safe. And, as the Jeep's engine roared to life, I remembered a line from my favourite Spider-Man comic: *"With great power there must also come great responsibility."*

I don't want to be no hero—fuck that. But still, deep down, I knew my war had just begun.

THE END

BERSERKER
GREEN HELL

A Lee Franklin Publication

http://www.leefranklin.com

Berserker: Green Hell
Author Notes

One of the many things I have learnt on my journey to becoming a published author is just how many pieces there are to a book, and all the work that goes into turning my ramblings and musings into sensible constructs.

I would really like to thank HellBound Books for their support – especially to James Longmore for pushing me to write a bigger story then I ever imagined existed, and, for such an amazing and painstaking job of editing. I promise I will learn how to use a comma... eventually!

To all my Beta readers – Denise Doyle and Donna Jensen, to name a couple of the many who have helped me in this journey by patiently traipsing through the quagmire of my manuscript to find the gems and cut loose the crap.

To Gail Beck, of the South West Aboriginal Land and Sea council, for her support and advice. I hoped to recognise the contribution of up to 500 Aboriginal and Torres Strait Islanders during the Vietnam War. As an incredible footnote from Australian history, it was only in 1967, the year in which the Vietnam War began, that our Aboriginal and Torres Strait Islanders won the

213

right to vote

and become recognised as Australian Citizens... a 'right' they earned forty thousand years before.

To the past, current, and future serving members of the Australian Defence Force. The very best and worst times of my life – Lest We Forget.

Unfortunately, the statistics for loss of life through US friendly fire are based on true documentation. This information was compiled by a US Army Captain, and has just recently found its way into the US national Archives and Records Administration to become a public document:
Friendly fire in Vietnam. Article from NY Times by CJ Chivers. FEB 18 2007

To my beautiful sons: Jacob, Santiago, & Ezequiel, who have supported and encouraged me every step of the way.

Finally, to my biggest fan and critic, Marcelo, without whom I would never dared believe I could write. You suffered and cheered every draft. You make my dreams come true every day.
Thank you is not a big enough word.

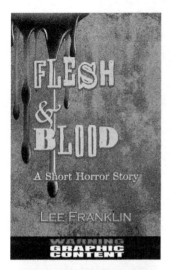

Kelly thought she knew who she was. Now, she is about to discover her own flesh and blood.

Torn from the only family she has known and sold to the highest bidder. Neglected, abused and tortured Mica discovers an appetite for revenge.

Blood is soaking the streets of Shawville this festive season. Residents are getting more than they bargained for at Laymon's Lot tree farm. Horror writers D.J. Doyle and Lee Franklin invite you into the darkest depths of their twisted psyches. From horny snowmen to flesh-eating elves, and the body count soaring, we encourage you to sit down, put your feet up, and allow us to disgust you with our depraved minds.
Countdown twelve days to a very bloody Xmas

Find more of Lee's short stories in these fantastic anthologies.

AVAILABLE ON AMAZON

AND KINDLE

Nang Tani

She Takes her Vengeance in Blood

A Novelette

Celebrating his twenty-first birthday in Thailand with his best mate Paul, Shane finds the perfect tattoo of a local deity, Nang Tani. He must have her at all costs. When Nang Tani is unleashed, she comes with vengeance. Shane will learn that sins, like tattoos, cannot be washed away; not even with blood.

Reviews for Nang Tani

"Holy brutality, Batman. This one took me by surprise. I had no idea what I was getting into, but I'm glad I gave it a shot. This is a story of brutal vengeance that kicks it into high gear about halfway through, and doesn't let up until the final word. I thoroughly enjoyed it, and I'll definitely be checking out more from this author." - Amazon Reviewer

"*Nang Tani* is an extreme and gruesome tale of deadly revenge that subverts the sexist tropes inherent in a lot of torture porn. It features a goddess that you don't pray to, you only pray you never, ever meet her." Jasper Bark - Author of *Stuck On You* and *The Final Cut*

"This story is just awesome, a tale of a forbidden tattoo and the curse that comes with it. So very good! I love revenge stories, this book is sick! Very satisfied with it!! 5/5 Tattooed Skulls." - Brad Tierney

Nang Tani - Rak Ruex

Coming Christmas '21

D.J. Doyle was raised by pot-smoking hippies and spent her days worshipping pagan deities in the Hell Fire Club and her nights watching horror movies and reading horror books. She now lives with her family in a treehouse, preying on unsuspecting travellers, and where she likes nothing better than coming up with ideas for new stories and plotting her next novel. Some of this might have been made up. To learn more about D.J. Doyle, you can visit her website or Facebook page.

Red - A serial killer with a taste for blood. Warning: This extreme horror is NOT for the fainthearted.

Occult Thriller/horror- A woman takes on the Druids to save her friend, and the world.

A Newgrange spinoff - 3 short stories about Father
Jack and his posse of priests.

Paranormal - A horror with some humour that is
drenched in Irish history and folklore.

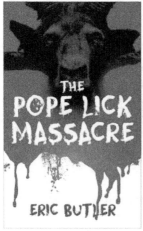

There are two types of people in Jefferson County: those who know the legend of the Pope Lick Monster and those who believe it. Before the night is over, Sam will have no choice but to join the believers.

Since their mother's death, Sam's sole focus has been taking care of her younger brother, Kenny. Now Kenny's Scout troop is missing, having never returned from the woods around Pope Lick.

Sam gathers a group of friends to search for the boys and their Scoutmaster. With each step, they get closer to discovering the scouts aren't the only ones in the woods this night.

"The Pope Lick Massacre is a bold, brutal horror story that'll remain in your mind long after you read it. This book is not for the faint of heart." – Independent Book Review